Denis EMORINE

DEATH AT HALF MAST

Novel

Denis EMORINE

DEATH AT HALF MAST

Novel

Translated from the French by Flavia Cosma
Translation edited by Denis Emorine and Michael
Todd Steffen
Foreword by Sonia Elvireanu
Footnotes and notes by Denis Emorine

Journal of Experimental Fiction 85

JEF Books/Depth Charge Publishing
Aurora, Illinois

Originally published as *La mort en berne*, 2017
Publisher: 5 Sens Éditions
Rue du Collège, 7
1227, Carouge (Suisse)
www.5senseditions.ch/index.html

Cover art: "Feuille d' automne" ("Autumn Leaf")
by Tatiana Samoïlova
www.tatiana-samoilova.com

ISBN 1-884097-85-5
ISBN-13 978-1-884097-85-0

ISSN 1084-547X

This volume is volume 85 of
The Journal of Experimental Fiction

JEF Books/Depth Charge Publishing
The Foremost in Innovative Fiction
Experimentalfiction.com

JEF Books are distributed to the book trade by
SPD: Small Press Distribution and to the
academic journal market by EBSCO

From the 5th to the 19th September 2016, the author benefited from a bursary in order to work and finish this novel at the writers' residence at Saorge Monastery–The National Monuments Centre, France,. Grateful thanks.

FOREWORD

Denis Emorine, *Death at Half-Mast* or The Romantic Auto Fiction

A French contemporary writer, translated and published in many countries, Denis Emorine explores various literary genres: poetry, theatre, novels, short stories, essays. For him the process of writing is a privileged space for reflecting on personal identity and questioning that identity. The identity quest of his creation, as defined by the principal character of the novel *Death at Half Mast*, finds its roots in the "Slavic atavism" of his Russian heritage.

The obsessive identity motif of his poems and plays is repeated in this autobiographical novel *Death at Half Mast*. This is an auto fiction, although the novel is written in the third person, having a narrator that is extradiegetic to the author, an alter ego, Dominique Valarcher.

The narrator acknowledges some aspects of the character's life that point to the life of the author himself (his social status) as a poet, playwright and novelist, whose works are well known abroad, is invited to read at conferences and to teach at foreign universities. The writer invents and fictionalizes sentimental and intellectual relations with his foreign

Denis Emorine

readers, and with young intellectual women.

The writer and his work are at the center of a novel, autobiographical and fictional at the same time. The protagonist is projected in the intimate universe of his creation, unveiling at the same time his own obsessions and the core of his work. He alludes to the subject of other short stories. He stages his relations with the process of writing, with editors and literary critics, through the story of his life, and his various encounters.

Dominique Valarcher is the man of a single love for Laetitia, the woman of his life, and without whom he is unable to imagine his life.

This novel makes it possible for the reader to better understand Denis Emorine's work: the quest for identity, the predilections of the intelligent and sensitive feminine characters, a certain type of woman (with physical and spiritual beauty, understanding and instincts to protect) a death obsession facing love, and even half-hearted lovemaking. At the same time, writing as therapy doesn't manage to heal the wound of the child who discovers at twelve years of age a family secret: his mother's love for her first husband, a Jew of Polish origins, dead very young at an Auschwitz concentration camp during the war. The faithfulness of the young woman in memory of her young husband seizes her with love for her child and his father. At twelve, a crushed identity becomes a wound that never heals, despite psychoanalysis. Writing is no more than a subterfuge for calming his demons with anamnesis, because loneliness and an obsession with death won't stop haunting the writer.

The narrator, alias author, unveils his tragic nature, due to his Eastern European identity, compatible with the tragic Russian child, the *Nitchevo*, defined by his "attitude of fatalism and resignation, characteristics of a Russian soul."[*]

Sonia Elvireanu

Poet, novelist critic, translator, reader at the Technical University of Cluj-Napoca, Romanian (doctor in Philology), cultural fellow at The French-Romanian Association AMI, Alba-Iulia; member of the Research Centre of the Imagining "Speculum" and Philosophical Research for Multicultural Dialog. University 1 December 1918, Alba-Iulia; member of the International Federation of French Teachers (FIPE), founder of the Francophone Cenacle "Jacques Prévert," Alba-Iulia.

Many thanks to Flavia, Sonia and Michael for your help. You've done a labor of love.

I wish to express my appreciation to Eckhard for his dedication. He was my publisher. Now, he is my friend.

With a huge hug.

Denis

My wish for beauty was much higher than my strength.

Pierre Reverdy

1

How did their story really begin? He couldn't say.

*

Those near him knew Dominique as an emotional and modest man. At times he could get uppity. He could overstep himself in heated debates with friends. High on the list of things he loved, he loved to write. Truth be told, beyond writing little else mattered to him. Now in his fifties, to his great satisfaction, he lived, as it were, by his plume. Without looking back, Dominique Valarcher left his job as a university librarian at the Sorbonne, where his wife Laetitia taught French literature and Latin.

His books were translated around Eastern Europe and in the United States. At times the writer had the impression of being better known outside his country, and this didn't bother him. However, France appeared to be waking up to him lately: he was invited to lecture at conferences. He had been granted writing residencies. "*Nobody is a prophet in his own land*" was an old saying especially fit for his case until the last couple of years. Dominique Valarcher had taken this late success in his country with a grain of salt and of course with certain satisfaction. Editors in America and Romania would offer him the privilege of publishing his poems or his plays in bilingual editions. The writer didn't ask for such favors. He had recently been invited to Benson College, a prestigious university in New York, an all-girls college that touted itself for educating of the most influential women in the world. Valarcher didn't think that studying French or even studying his own books would prepare these girls very well for the afore-mentioned task, but he was flattered by the fact that this prestigious, very selective university would pay him this homage this way. He would have been happy to be able to practice speaking English with the students but the American Professor, Jim Cole, warned him: No English in the foreign language and civilization classes. The rule was very strict. And in this establishment where the best of the best were recruited to teach, they didn't mess around with the rules.

Valarcher had been invited for a week at Benson College in extremely advantageous conditions. The writer realized during that year that he might be able to abandon his work without any inconvenience at 51 years of age, something unhoped for. At the University, the man in charge of the French language and literature department welcomed him with these simple words: "Hi, Dominique! How's the Eiffel Tower? Are its feet still cold?" [1]

The typically American ease of the salutation didn't baffle our writer, who smiled and answered without losing a beat, "Theoretically no. I bought her two pairs of slippers before leaving!" His answer made the gathering of students and professors laugh. Cole was teaching French here in exceptionally good conditions: approximately a dozen students in each class, a lot of money invested in educational material, young, cultured women, and hand-picked on top of everything. The selection was pitiless: many students, even from privileged families, had to borrow heavily to be admitted into the holy of holies. How could one fail to assure quality teaching in these conditions?

The students watched the writer with great attention. Toasts were made. Everyone seemed familiar with his new books, which amazed him. Well, life was beautiful! *God bless America.* [2]

Back in his small village in the Ile-de-France,

---

[1] Allusion to *Paris s'éveille, a* song by the French singer Jacques Dutronc.

[2] In English in the original.

he was pleased to find a calmer atmosphere. Laetitia welcomed him by saying simply, "I've missed you."

Grisette, the cat, didn't even look at him. This was a manner of saying to its master that nothing had changed while he was absent and that life had gone routinely on, at least for the feline. Indeed, students' papers to be corrected, books about naturalism and others, piled up on his wife's busy desk. No, nothing had changed, except that from now on he'd be handing in his resignation as a librarian at the Sorbonne. What a joyful thought! He had dreamt of this for such a long time! The change took place without any problems. He wouldn't be constrained to follow regular hours any more, that's all. To be able to dedicate his time to his work, wouldn't that be the most wonderful freedom of all, an unquestionable sign of his achievement? Dominique Valarcher had always thought life was the opposite of work, which all those years back he believed he loved and which, with the passing of years, had changed into something strictly necessary for survival.

*

A little after his trip to New York, he received a message from a young Hungarian student, Nora Nemeth. She corresponded by mail with an American girl studying at Benson. Rebecca Wilson spoke to her enthusiastically about Dominique Valarcher's visit to the University. Obviously, he had made a strong impression on the students as well as on their professors. Rebecca Wilson? That name didn't ring a bell. Nora, who wasn't familiar with his work, researched on the internet, visited the writer's site and read a few of his poems and plays. Rebecca had sent her Dominique's most recent books. Nora was thinking about doing a Master's thesis in French on Valarcher. And for this purpose, she dared to contact him directly. The title of her thesis would be *The Estranged Dominique Valarcher: Romanticism and Heartbreak.*

Nora was seeking his seal of approval on the theme before starting the work. Attached to the letter she'd sent a photo. Valarcher took a moment to contemplate the face with harmonious traits which disturbingly resembled the actress Tatiana Samoilova. When he was a child, Dominique Valarcher saw the Russian movie *The Cranes Are Flying (Quand Passent les Cigognes)* on a French TV station. He must have been around 10 then. It was during the sixties. The Russian movie had received the Palme d'Or at the Cannes' Festival in 1958. The child didn't understand

Denis Emorine

everything, of course, though he was definitely charmed by the young woman's interpretation. He saw her in his dreams; she smiled at him, took him into her arms, talking to him in an unknown language with melodious inflections that made him tingle. Nora was like an incarnation of the Russian actress to whom, a few years back, he had dedicated a poem that she would never read.

To Tatiana Samoïlova

The street you live on
Narrows more and more
It deadens walkers' steps,
Passers-bye lost in a past.
A little child lost his way too
Amid the dirty snow-banks that overran
Your neighborhood.

In vain you clean
The steamed windows of your house
One cannot distinguish anything outside.
At times a solitary passer-bye slows his pace
But with a gesture of your hand
You sweep him away from your horizon

Tatiana,
It would be much better to stop whispering your name
Since the little boy doesn't recognize you anymore.
Your life is out of breath
Silence has become a misunderstood realm
You are looking for the bottle of oblivion
But someone stole it from you
Instead of taking you by the hand

When the night is falling, Moscow disappears
Don't open the window, Tatiana,
Don't you see that everyone has left
Taking your beauty with them far from here?
You won't be able to soar again.
Let alone this little boy
Leave him to lament his past
Yours disappeared long ago
In vain you clean
The steamed windows of your life
The horizon wears away
Under the pressure of your hand.

It was rumored that Tatiana Samoilova had given in to alcohol and drugs because her international career was crushed by the Soviet Union, left sinking in lonely old age, wholly forgotten. For Dominique, the actress had remained Veronika, Boris's passionate bride-to-be, the beautiful leading star of a movie that had troubled him so much. When in 2014 he found out that she had died, strangely enough he suffered as if he had known her very well. A part of his childhood disappeared with her passing. He went searching feverishly for her photos on the Internet and printed some before furiously destroying them a few days after.

The Estranged one? Romanticism and Heartbreak? Yes, it was exactly his portrait; Nora Nemeth had found the perfect expression. She found *the right words.*

He glanced again at her photo on the screen of the computer. Once again he was fascinated by that resemblance. Nora was beautiful: the student had a large brow, hair black and thick, eyes shaped like almonds and her face had the regular traits of *his* Tatiana, like and like. How could this be? Thoughtful, the writer turned off the computer. Still he needed to think, although his decision had been made.

Valarcher was about to name his older daughter Veronika, but changed his mind at the last moment, renouncing it as foolishly sentimental. He didn't dare talk to Laetitia about this matter, thinking without doubt, but maybe being wrong, that his wife wouldn't understand. Laetitia was a very rational woman, contrary to her husband, and this fact gave a relative stability to their lives as a couple. Their two daughters, Natacha and Laure, took after their mother. The parents saw them rarely now because the girls were working abroad. Natacha, the eldest was working in IT within an international company in Frankfort, and Laure was working at a London Bank. Neither of them read a single line of the books written by Dominique Valarcher. They showed serene indifference—or so it seemed—for their father's creativity. When he was younger, the writer was affected by this. Maybe it was his hurt pride? It was as it was though; he didn't understand why this happened. Dominique was certain that if his father or his mother had been writers or artists he would have been very proud of them. His children's lack of interest seemed to him almost against nature. The girls simply never manifested any desire to talk about his art to their father, or to ask him a single question about his books. This stung the paternalistic pride of Dominique Valarcher, but he refrained from asking for justifications. That's the way it was, though, he just had to accept it. In his innocence, the writer imagined that a father of girls wasn't a man like any other and would have a privileged relationship with them. This was another pipe dream!

*

Nora's interest touched him deeply because of their age difference. The young Hungarian girl could have been his daughter. The student loved his work and she was twenty-three like Laure his daughter, being at the same time the spitting image of Tatiana Samoilova. More wasn't necessary for Dominique, *the romantic and the estranged,* to become exalted. It was certainly ridiculous, and so what? He was perfectly aware of this, while he tried hard to delay answering the young girl's letter with the enthusiasm of an adolescent. For now, he wouldn't say a word about this to Laetitia knowing pertinently that he would do it sooner or later. With difficulty the writer resisted the urge to turn his computer back on and contemplate the photo of the young girl.

Valarcher went out to the garden, walked a few steps here and there. He loved these moments of solitude. It was the end of winter. The air was a little frisky. The garden, yet sleepy, would soon blossom. All of the greenery would appear again. He took his time gazing around at the trees and grass. He felt wonderful, certainly. How to put it better? In harmony with himself; this didn't happen so often.

*

Laetitia's return brought him back to reality, out of his thoughts. His wife smiled at him from afar waving her hand, before parking the car into the old barn which served as a garage. They had met at the Faculty of Letters, in Paris. The young man felt love at first sight for this literature student whom he had met during a French class. She was reserved, didn't ever mix with the others, and this immediately seduced him. With a timid nature, Dominique had a hard time confiding in others. The student, crazy for literature and romantic poetry, had shown her a few poems that he composed; he was so in need to conquer her admiration! Laetitia wouldn't confide in others. She proved as a confidante to be discreet and attentive, two qualities that Dominique had always appreciated, and which he possessed in his turn. When the young girl revealed that she liked his inspiration, he threw himself at her feet. Nothing more. What else could he do? He didn't have a clue. Dominique had ended by shyly unveiling his sentiments: "I really like you."

She smiled a little. At that moment the young man understood that this was his woman, no, THE Woman of his life. Then he read her one of his latest poems that started something like this:

In the beauty of your radiant hair,
–Death at half-mast–
I forget the devastation of the world.
I live on the balcony of the stars,
–those keepers of dead loves' blood–
I will draw on the sky
The groove of our joined hands
Thanking you

All is accomplished...

Laetitia didn't laugh at these verses streaming with clumsy tenderness, verses he never showed to anybody before. She found them beautiful and she muttered something deploring their sadness. She didn't dare formulate this objection in front of the young man who held to the old notion of courtly love. He courted her as in the old days. The young girl sensed even then that his shyness sheltered a sensitive and passionate temperament that was far from displeasing her.   She was afraid to hurt him, understandably. A single poem stammered by this young student and poet so different from the others was enough for Laetitia to realize the character of the man who would share a life with her. He would be the chosen one and nobody else.

2

That night, leaving the young girl that fascinated him, Dominique had a single thought: "I think she loves me because she loves what I write."

Death at half mast, the student took a long walk along the city streets he identified with his love. He didn't need to live on the balcony of the stars any longer; they approached Dominique close enough they almost touched him. They signaled to him flickering solely for him. Love and eternity took Laetitia's visage; a name predestined for a girl studying classic literature and being his lover. Occasionally fate displayed the face of happiness even if its etymology was a heresy. After all, wasn't it Homer who said the future lay the lap of the gods?

*

Back then Laetitia wore her chestnut hair back, flowing down to her shoulders and thick, with red ribbons, because combs slipped and wouldn't stay put. During a trip to Florence, some years later, he gave her some ivory combs. Life smiled at them. They adored Italy. So many years later, Dominique still needed to take refuge in his lover's arms. The young lovers married and had been living together since she was twenty and he was twenty three. Twenty three...was exactly Laure's and Nora Nemeth's age. Was it only a coincidence? He didn't think so, because in the realm of sentiments there isn't such a thing. Everything was determined, and especially lovers' first encounters.

He turned on the computer and reread Nora's message written in perfect French:

> *Dear Sir,*
> *My name is Nora Nemeth*
> *Please forgive me for taking the liberty to write this*
> *Without being introduced to you.*
> *I am a French student at the University of Pecs, in Hungary.*

Why wait? Her words were beautiful in their simplicity:

> *Dear Nora* (his age allowed for this familiarity surely!)
> *Your spontaneity delights me.*
> *I am honored that you appreciate my writings.*
> *I am at your disposal if you have any questions about my work. Feel free to ask.*
> *I would be pleased to help.*

Cordially yours
Dominique Valarcher

"Thrilled," "very honored," and "enchanted." Wasn't this rather hyperbolic vocabulary? Too bad. After all, *dear Nora* possessed the enthusiasm of youth. This French writer wasn't that insensitive to that. He shouldn't deceive her. He sent the message without rereading it and rubbed his hands. Tatiana Samoilova wasn't dead; she had been reincarnated and was named Nora Nemeth. This enigma excited Dominique.

*

Dominique Valarcher wasn't always a patient person. He waited impatiently for the young girl's answer. He documented himself on Nora's University imagining her life there in Pecs as a studious student. He and Laetitia had visited Budapest some years ago, as a romantic couple. They had reserved a ship-hotel on the quays of the Danube but Pecs didn't evoke anything for him.

One more reason to get some idea of this town "animated by the laughter of the students" as a well-known French guide put it. The writer's imagination was galloping. He could see Nora with French books in hand, accompanied by young people her own age, visiting the library of her University and discovering the books of a certain Dominique Valarcher....Had she ever read *The Public Lobby* (*La salle des pas perdus*), one of his best plays, that alluded at the encounter of a young girl and an enigmatic middle age man on a train-station quay? Or had she read his latest poetry collection *Storms. The Unfinished Score* (*Tempête. La partition inachevée*), with the dedication of many poems to Soviet writers and artists imprisoned and deported under Stalin? She hadn't mentioned this. He'd have to wait.

A while ago, Jean-François Macor, a reputed French Press director, had asked him for a manuscript. It would be a collection of short stories. He'd been working on the project for several months.

Days passed. The writer waited in vain for a sign of Nora. Why this silence? He'd answered her more than a week ago.... Though normally talkative, he didn't reveal anything about this to his wife. It is true that Laetitia looked worried as of late. Dominique remembered Mrs Ibrahim, his former philosophy teacher in the Senior year as a High School Literature major.

"Teaching is a neurosis!"

Some jeers were heard in the class. Dominique alone smiled back at her. The high-school students approved of these words, wondering at the same time how somebody could reveal the darker side in front of the students.

His mother, an English teacher at a college in the suburbs of Paris, spent hours and hours preparing classes and correcting students' papers, and busied herself at the same time with Dominique's homework. His father, of a far-off Russian ascendancy, had transmitted to his son a sensibility, excessive at times. His parents had died two years apart, some years ago, and this sank the writer into a deep depression he still had not climbed back out of, he was certain. He consulted many psychiatrists without any luck. "You have to accept it," one of them advised him, with an erudite tone. To accept? No, never. The writer stood up in a hurry, threw a few bills on the desk and didn't ever see that incompetent practitioner again, in his opinion a charlatan. Happily it didn't take long for him to be introduced to a new psychiatrist, Doctor Samuel Bronstein, warmly recommended by a lady friend. His method, based on dialogue, was more appropriate for Dominique.

In one of his novels, the main protagonist,

with whom Dominique identified himself, exclaimed with bitterness, "One never learns how to be an orphan and that's a curse. Not being prepared for the death of one's mother and father is one of the great failures of education. The education that we receive and give to our kids makes a lot of victims, in this respect."

*

Finally the long awaited answer arrived. Nora thanked him very much for his kindness. Obviously she had read a good part of his work. The professor responsible for her Masters accepted the premise of the thesis. The student, of course, would have some questions for him. She was swamped with work but would write more soon. Dominique repeated that he was at her disposal and wished her all the best.

*

For a long time, Laetitia and Dominique had merged as though they constituted just a single being. When they met they were very young, studying in Paris. They shared a lot of secrets, even if Laetitia, being more discreet, opened her heart less than her companion. This time around, in a curious way, he hadn't spoken to her about the Hungarian student, without understanding why very clearly. Dominique's sentiments about paternity didn't change; he was under the impression that their two daughters shared more with their mother than with him and this hurt him, although he never revealed this to his wife but he was certain that she must have known about it. He was convinced—despite all evidence—that a daughter by nature seeks her father's compassion. But he was soon disillusioned; it was far from the case with Natacha and Laure. As children and even adolescents they confided naturally in their mother, seeking her affections. They spoke more readily to her. Whenever Laetitia was absent, which rarely happened, the two girls displayed a serene indifference regarding their father; they wouldn't include him in their discussions. He would have loved to have been asked his advice in choosing a dress, for them to have opened their hearts to him a little...though they did not. He was always under the impression of being an intruder and felt animosity from them, even though he kept his thoughts to himself.

Laure and Natacha, aged respectively twenty-three and twenty-eight, now saw their parents more rarely than before, maybe at Christmas. Dominique didn't really suffer after the girls left home—at least he tried to persuade himself of this—but he had this tendency of considering young girls that he happened to appreciate more, like his own symbolic daughters, without starting an ambiguous relationship with them. He realized this fact one day when one of his readers, transformed into friend, confided to him that she would have liked him to be her father. This revelation wasn't disagreeable; on the contrary, he was even touched by it, but after, Diane decided to tell him a story—her more than disappointing "first time" with a guy. Without being shocked, he told her that she shouldn't honor him with such a confidence because his quality as a writer didn't make a therapist out of him for all that. Diane replied brusquely that she didn't consider him as a psychiatrist but more like the father she had chosen for herself; her parents had divorced when she was five years old and her real father didn't have much to do with her. Diane felt hate for the spouse of her mother, incapable of assuming his paternity.

"Your daughters must be so proud of you!" she added, hurting him without wanting to.
She took him by the arm, but the hurt was still there. No, his daughters weren't proud of him but indifferent towards his writing career and he suffered much at the same time trying to keep this pain all to

himself. Dominique stood quiet. He had to listen to the whole long story of this sexual experience that nevertheless was trying for Diane and the word was feeble. When she started crying, he took her simply in his arms, very moved, caressing her hair. He thought that his spontaneous reaction towards Diane would have certainly shocked Natacha and Laure but he didn't feel at all guilty. After all the father and the man didn't need justification for an affectionate gesture. Diane had given him nice proof of confidence although her story was embarrassing. She whispered a few words in his ear that he preferred not to remember. Dominique accepted the role of a confidante, not without a certain smug self-complacency but with good will.

Laetitia knew that her husband always preferred feminine friendships; he never hid this. He had always disliked the masculine world and its implicit rules. Apparently his wife didn't formulate her thoughts about this, but they didn't talk about it. Being reserved by nature, Dominique never asked her. Nevertheless, recently his "girl" friends ranged in their vast majority between the ages of twenty and thirty, being usually his readers. In their opinion, the heroines of his novels and plays were "truer," "more endearing" and "more sensible" than their masculine counterparts, much more superficial and helpless.

Carol Mendoza, a Mexican student at Benson College, had written a brilliant exposé on his work. She demonstrated that Dominique Valarcher was evidently a feminist because his heroes were "without exception, cowards who were running away from their responsibilities most of the time." Him, a feminist? Valarcher wasn't sure about that, even if the supposed masculine values left him indifferent, or even hostile. He didn't recognize himself in the portrait-robot displayed at length in magazines and revues that showed a man obsessed by social climbing, power, and conquering women. He judged them very caricature-like and off the mark when applied to him. In fact Dominique had always wanted to have girls, contrary to Laetitia who affirmed that she didn't have any preferences.

Carol Mendoza analyzed the theme of romanticism in his play *The Public Lobby* (*La salle des pas perdus*). She saw in the masculine character a protective father, which was without doubt true; Dominique voluntarily agreed. The students wanted to know if he was inspired by true people in describing the psychology of the two characters of the play. When Dominique admitted that he, the omniscient writer, didn't know, they suspected a deliberate evasion on his part but they didn't insist. When he answered affirmatively to the question "Do you have any daughters?" they smiled and looked at each other with a triumphant air. The cause was now understood: the French writer was a specialist in the feminine psyche, a *rara avis* in the masculine literary world, briefly, a beautiful symbol of the *French Touch.* Dominique didn't dare contradict them. The students wouldn't believe him anyway. This flattering repute, even seized upon, was all to his advantage. *Vanitas vanitatum et omnia vanitas.* The Ecclesiast was apparently right.

At the end of the week spent at Benson College, William Cole expressed his great satisfaction; the young girls had much appreciated the man and the writer.

"To be continued, Dominique.... Keep in touch!" [3] the professor said, vigorously shaking his hand. *"Be well and keep at it!"* [4]

---

[3]   In English in the original.

[4]   In English in the original.

After all these years, Laetitia and Dominique had remained fond of one another. Was it something really exceptional? Their friends and acquaintances said yes, it was. They would not even ask themselves this question. Dominique spoke often about Laetitia as of the woman to whom he belonged without restrictions. The fusion-like relationship of their youth transformed itself into reciprocal tenderness. At times Dominique Valarcher would observe Laetitia from afar, bent over her copies. She would lift her head, the red pen suspended in the air, before continuing with her corrections, with an absorbed air. He wouldn't be able to live without her, was it so difficult to understand? If their passion stirred an enigma in the world's eyes, too bad, or all the better!

The writer had a hard time concentrating on this manuscript of short stories, as if he had detached himself from his work. Luckily, when telephoning, Jean-Francois Macor wasn't pushing him too hard.

"Take your time," he would say. "Promise me simply to give me your next book. Your word is enough. Short stories? Perfect. If you are coming to Paris, pay me a visit, why don't you? I'll introduce some colleagues to you, and we could go eat together,

OK? You don't have a very restrictive contract with your regular editor, do you? Will he accept this small infidelity without having a jealous fit?" And he would burst out laughing as if it was all a good joke for his fellow man of letters. The Editor's warm voice and his sense of humor seduced the writer right away.

Dominique promised that yes he would answer positively to this invitation. Jean-Francois Macor revealed himself an agreeable interlocutor and a man to reckon with.

Dominique sighed. For the first time, he had doubts about himself. Would he be able to still write from now on? Was it a good idea to start back with the short stories? He hadn't written short fiction in six years at least. Would it be better to go on to other things? He could easily announce his decision to Jean-Francois Macor, who seemed like an understanding editor. He was about to take the phone from the hook but immediately changed his mind. No short stories, OK but with what to replace them? No, better wait a little. The inspiration will appear. It was a matter of time, as his new editor affirmed. After all, since the editor solicited the writer it was because he knew his work well enough. Even more, Macor had an excellent reputation, evidently justified. He was very demanding about the quality of the manuscripts he was publishing.

The day went by quietly. Dominique was preoccupied without really admitting it. He stood up and went into the garden. The cat was playing with a bird. Grisette startled when it heard the sliding door closing with a sharp noise, and after continued its carousel as if nothing had happened. The writer watched it from afar abstaining to intervene. At the Valarcher's the cats weren't deprived of their prey just because the humans felt obliged to do so and severely judge the "cat's cruelty." The collar with a bell supposed to alert the bird of the danger was equally prohibited. Laetitia and he considered this practice hypocritical and ridiculous. He whispered, "Come on, Grisette didn't need sympathy, neither did he for that matter."

*

The following days, Dominique Valarcher restarted his work without too much difficulty. He hadn't ever known about that thing familiarly called *writer's block* although he had a strong sense of "the anguish connected with the empty page" in certain circumstances. Truth to be told, nothing pressed him.

Paradoxically, the easiness of Jean-Francois Macor turned out to be stimulating. The editor was without a doubt a fine psychologist, a quality far off from this profession!

Nora sent him another message with a long list of questions, excusing herself at the same time for bothering him. Dominique Valarcher answered assuring her that he would respond with pleasure. She informed him that Erika Somogyi, the director of the French Studies Department of her University, would write to him personally, if that was okay. She wanted the writer to give at least two Conferences in Pecs, one about his poetry and the other about contemporary French literature. The writer answered that he would accept the invitation with pleasure, if he was available. In the immediate future, he didn't have any projects in the United States or anywhere else; it would be perfect. The thought of going to Hungary to visit an unknown city seduced him.

Immediately he received a message from Erika Somogyi. He would stay for a week in Pecs. It would be sufficient for him to give the two conferences, meeting professors and students and maybe organizing some writing workshops. Probably by the end of April. She warned him that he wouldn't be paid for this, but that the costs of travel and staying over would be covered by the University. He accepted. The writer had more than a month to prepare. This perspective enchanted him: he would get to meet Nora.

3

Dominique Valarcher's plane landed at Pecs-Pogany airport on the 19th of April, early in the afternoon. He went straight to the exit. He saw a man with a poster with his name who gave Dominique a piece of paper; Erika excused herself for not being able to set herself free as anticipated because of a last minute interview which she couldn't avoid. A taxi would take the writer directly to the students' neighborhood where he could deposit his bags and install himself in the apartment attributed to him on Sausage Avenue a few meters from the University. Erika or Nora would get in touch with him in approximately one hour. The weather was mild that day. His Tourist Guide qualified Pecs as *a Mediterranean town with a singular charm, benefiting from a microclimate.* In his room Dominique found a few brochures in French and English and also a bottle of Zweigelt, a renowned red vine from the region. Nora had written him a few words:

> *It is very good, you'll see!*
>
> *Welcome to Hungary Mr. Valarcher!*
>
> *Your student,*
>
> *Nora.*

He was had just finished a shower and was dressing in a new suit when he heard a tapping at the door.

"It's Nora." He heard a melodious and slightly veiled voice with a slight accent. He opened the door quickly. The young girl smiled. Her likeness with Tatiana Samoilova was even more astonishing in real life than in the photograph. Dominique was troubled....He didn't know what to say for a moment but recovered quickly.

"Please come in, Nora. I was impatient to meet you."

"Me too," she answered. "It's a great pleasure to meet with you. You know, I really like your writing!"

"It's an honor for me that you chose me for your Masters. I don't know how to thank you," said the writer.

Nora stepped into the room.

"As I told you, Rebecca gave me your new books as a present. I visited your site on the Internet as well. I also tele-charged the recording of your conferences in the United States, in French and English...some interviews in literary magazines.... It was wonderful for me. If you aren't too tired from your trip, we could take a tour of the city, have a bite to eat somewhere. In any case if you allow me I'll be your guide during your stay."

The writer gladly accepted. Nora was open. She was a good French speaker. He gave her a little parcel.

"A small, typically French gift for you."

After opening the parcel, she smiled at him.

"Perfume!" exclaimed the girl. "What a beautiful surprise!"

"I hope you will love it," answered the writer. "I picked it up *Diorella,* the perfume my younger daughter prefers, and she is your age."

"I love all French perfumes and Dior the most, like this one!"

Her eyes sparkled. Nora took the writer by the arm.

"Let's go! You absolutely need to discover this city. You'll see it's so beautiful! I was born here, you know. It's part of me. Let's go have a drink at the cafe Paulus, a favorite hangout of the students."

The cafe was full. A happy brouhaha welcomed them. Some young people greeted Nora, who introduced Dominique Valarcher to them, *a great French writer.* She seemed proud to be by his side. A student asked him for an autograph; another showed him a poetry collection he dedicated to Laetitia, written five years ago.

"I adored this," she exclaimed. "Your wife is very lucky! I would love to receive praises like this."

Embarrassed, the writer blushed without answering.

Valarcher was feeling good. The town was dominated by a mysterious charm, was *animated by the laughter of the students*, as a consecrated expression went. All of the travelers' guides were talking about Pecs in glowing, unalterable terms, but they didn't exaggerate.

The sojourn passed way too fast for his taste. It is true that his program left him much time for exploring the city in Nora's company. This was the idea, Erika Somogyi had warned him. It was important that *our writer* (this familiarity enchanted Dominique) would impregnate himself with the spirit of this town, *one of the pearls of Hungary*, in her view.

With the Hungarian student as a guide, he couldn't ask for more.

*

The conference about *French Contemporary Literature, directives and beginnings*, and the other consecrated to his poetic work attracted a lot of students. When, at Nora's insistence, he took up to speak about his career as a writer, he decided to read a few excerpts from his books—poems, a short story, a fragment from his latest play—before letting voluntary students speak. The dialogue started; it was very lively. Nora spoke enthusiastically about her Masters, insisting on the author's romanticism *and* on that *fracture* she had discerned in his books.

"The search for a ruptured identity passes through the books of Dominique Valarcher," she stated with a lump in her throat. "Each of his works tries hard to reconstruct this identity. Each of them is a piece of an unfinished puzzle which we may wonder if the author wishes really to solve." When a student asked him how he planned to finish the puzzle, Dominique answered that "only death would take care of this." This revelation was met by some disapproving murmurs. Dominique had the impression that part of the audience was shocked by it, so he hurried up to add that he wasn't disposed to wait until death would decide for him and that he would oppose it with determination. He didn't accept defeat; he'd fight it until the end. Much applause resonated for a long time in the amphitheatre and the writer smiled for the assistants. Nora was watching him with a certain melancholy in her eyes. He promised himself to ask her the reason but then decided not to. After all, maybe he deluded himself, that expression was extremely fugitive. Why succumb to the curiosity and take the risk of disconcerting the young girl?

*

The last night in Pecs, Nora and Dominique walked the streets for a long time after an intimate diner in a small restaurant that specialized in Hungary's traditional cuisine, nested near the cathedral. They ate a delicious pörkölt* chatting non-stop about the future of Europe and Nora's future. Nora thought that he was very lucky for living in France; he agreed. Nora inquired if his two daughters were happy in a foreign country. Dominique realized that this question was puzzling to him because he wasn't capable of answering it. For an instant, sadness invaded him. He stopped short of taking her hand and kissing it. The particularly mild weather was suitable for long walks. Valarcher looked at the statue of Franz Liszt mounted in his balcony, at Széchenyi Square. After greeting the musician with exaggerated reverence—a gesture that much amused the student— he suggested Nora call him by his name, Dominique,

36

"simply Dominique." Nora leaned her head on his shoulder. He wanted this moment of abandonment to last forever. Neither of them moved.... Finally the young girl slowly raised her head and smiled at him. Her beauty subjugated him. He couldn't take his eyes away from her face. Nora blushed slightly and turned her eyes away. All of the sudden, Dominique thought he would like to die in this place, far from his home. At the last minute, he stopped himself for imparting this confidence to the young lady. No, what a crazy idea! He shouldn't say it, definitely not! This morbid thought would in truth hurt the sensibility of the young lady and could spoil everything. When Dominique was a child, his father one day told him never to linger around a moment of great happiness, because you couldn't be sure of ever reliving that moment again. Dominique didn't dare ask his father if leaving meant dying in his mind, but the sadness that he saw in his father's eyes, and which dissipated in an instant, didn't leave doubts regarding the subject. The writer remembered another sibylline phrase: "I am on a reprieve from the time of the German occupation."

Many years later, he understood his father's circumlocution. This revelation was painful.

Dominique's obsession with death had profound causes and not only these....

As a Russian francophone literary critic, Igor Zourine put it, the Slavic atavism impregnated his work.

"Your Russian side troubles me," Laetitia revealed one day with emotion, after reading one of his particularly somber short stories. "Where does this obsession with death come from? It's feeding and destroying you at the same time? Your father didn't seem as desperate as this, though...."

Romanticism and heartbreak, the student wrote....The portrait was true: she found the right words. When she asked Dominique to recite a poem for her, he excused himself, pretending that he didn't know any by heart. The student seemed disappointed but kept her silence. Maybe she didn't believe him. He felt hurt; it was the truth, though, but why justify oneself? Hand in hand, they walked on silently, for a while, through the sleeping town...

They decided they would see each other again soon, maybe in France this time. Nora asked him if he might send her something he'd been working on recently, some unpublished manuscripts perhaps.... Dominique accepted gladly. That night a young lady in blossom had chosen him, perched on the balcony of the stars. Songs of newer friendships rose into the Hungarian night vibrating exclusively just for them. No, he wasn't about to die. Not yet. He was also in reprieve but the last piece of the puzzle had to wait. Dominique didn't deem himself defeated. That night death wouldn't come from the East. At least not yet.

*

Back home, Dominique Valarcher soon found the thread of his short-stories: fracture in its different aspects. He rubbed his hands. The editor will be content, thought Dominique. He would start working, at peace finally. When Laetitia inquired if he was satisfied with his trip, he answered evasively mentioning Erika and Nora, the students he'd met, and finished by saying that he would gladly return to Pecs, with her the next time. He affirmed that he was subjugated by that city's charm. She believed him without a doubt and accepted his proposal with no hesitation. His enthusiasm was highly contagious.

He received a cheerful message from Nora:

I miss you.

I had a wonderful time in your company.

I use the perfume every day, thinking of you, Dominique!

Please forgive me; you must think that I am insolent speaking to you like this!

Nora

No, he didn't find her insolent. On the contrary, her freshness enchanted him.

He affirmed this in his message and finished it like this:

See you very soon, I hope, dear, dear Nora

I am at your disposal

Hugs

Yours Dominique

*

Dominique Valarcher restarted his work on the manuscript with pleasure. His Hungarian escapade had been good for him. The expression *broken identity* used by Nora hit him the hardest. She *was more than pertinent.* When he was 12, the writer was confronted by a family secret of which he never spoke to anyone, relieving it perhaps in an unconscious way in his writing. His mother born in 1919 had married once before. At 20 years of age she married a Frenchman of Polish origins, Jewish by his mother, Dinah Rosental. Under German occupation Paul Barbier was deported at Auschwitz in 1942 and died there a few weeks before the Soviets liberated the camp.

One day when his parents weren't home, while rummaging through the old desk of their room, little Dominique found some intimate papers: the letters of that man to his mother, a few photographs of them together, some documents with a swastika on them...A dozen of almost faded out lines gave him a shock. Barbier wanted their first child to be named Dominique! When his mother had a boy by her second husband, she then respected the wishes of the deceased. Dominique Valarcher didn't utter a word to anybody about this and most of all not to his mother. Did Camille Valarcher know that her only child had been informed about this matter? He was never able to take the first step, to interrogate his mother on this tragedy. How could he? At twelve the young boy was under the impression that he had lost his childhood forever, especially his innocence. On a symbolic level, he was the child of that man, which was why they gave him an androgynous name. [5] Another Paul Barbier

---

[5] In French, *Dominique* is a sexless name.

letter unveiled the fact that he would have liked to have a girl.

The letter ended by an alexandrine verse: "*Our love continue like the wind within the trees.*" Dominique started hating the deceased with all his might, that lucky chosen one who robbed him of his motherly love and dispossessed his father. The young boy had a hard time resisting the urge to destroy that hideous correspondence. He simply didn't understand. Nobody else but his father deserved that love. Sometimes, at night Dominique woke up crying. In his delirious state he would hear a masculine voice pronouncing his name and his mother's name, snickering.

During that time the boy wondered if his legitimate father knew the truth. Dominique went through a grave interior crisis that lasted some years and from which he never really recovered, except by the way of writing, more or less. He understood why one day his mother confided in him with great emotion, to the effect that she would have preferred a girl although she adored her little Dominique. In that instant perhaps, the child should have opened his heart and told her, but he felt chained by the revelation. In a way he carried his mother and that man's past like carrying a cross. Dominique never stopped being overwhelmed.

Broken identity.... Yes, and to what extent! Maybe someday he could confide in Nora? He was seduced by this idea but it was too early; to be honest, he didn't know anything or very little about the girl except that touching freshness of her and the admiration she had for his work. Was that enough to start telling her his family's secrets, a confession for which she wasn't prepared? How would she take this confidence from a man old enough to be her father? Dominique didn't ignore that sometimes this symbolism appeared heavier in consequences than one would suppose at the beginning.... Allowing himself to go along with this impulse would be the proof of his egocentrism.

Nora was the same age as Laure of course, but at least for now, her relationships with the writer were strictly "professional" and not affective. Dominique deplored this, selfishly.

*

Laetitia arrived back home. He heard her parking the car in front of the house. He needed her tenderness so much. Sometimes Dominique loved to throw himself into her arms suddenly, and often wondered if she felt the same. Valarcher was always taken by surprise by these sentiments he felt for his wife. Sometimes she unsettled him by her reserved attitude. In a popular psychology magazine, the writer had read that in an amorous relationship one of the two—the one who suffers—loves the other more, he is more romantic, more exalted and dissatisfied, watching out for the other nonstop and imploring for proof of love while the other has a calmer relationship, made of serene certitudes. He was wondering at times if their relationship offered an accurate representation of this theory. Many times he would have liked her to be the one to precipitate towards him, to embrace him tenderly, to nestle her head on his shoulder and let go but she would rarely behave like this, hardly ever as a matter of fact.

When she entered the room he kept watching the screen of his computer, pretending he didn't hear her coming in. What would she do? His wife approached him and smiled.

"The day is over," she said.

Was it enough? He wondered. *Love, was this love?* He would have liked to interrogate her about her definition of passion, about the idea she had regarding their *love.* But he didn't. Who had said that

"Love doesn't exist; there is only proof of love"? He didn't remember now. It didn't matter. Oh, yes, it was Pierre Reverdy, one of his favorite poets.

He kept his eyes on his page, pretending he was carefully reading the last lines of his text, which he erased automatically; then he thought of Nora one more time. Laetitia wouldn't be fooled by his small trick, but once again she didn't comment.

*

Dominique Valarcher thought himself a very complicated man.

*

He was content to have found his inspiration. Longer that he thought at the start, the novel he was writing at that moment told the story of a man still young who had lost his woman and couldn't get hold of himself. One day an unknown woman moved into the next apartment; her name was Patricia like his former wife; she used the same perfume—in fact there were resemblances betweenthe two—and this woman ended up invading his life without being invited to do so. The writer described in details the decline of this man at the time of their meeting and the way the mysterious seductress one by one destroyed the memories linked with his first love. It was at the same time a resurrection and a descent into hell. Were these things that incompatible? This text was a sort of tentative answer. At first the writer thought of naming the work *The Spider* or *The Predator*. Finally, he thought each title, more and more suggestive, would preclude any surprise for the reader. On the other hand Dominique was afraid that out of analogy *The Spider* would bring to mind Clarimonde, the evil creature of Hans Heinz Ewers. It would be better to preserve some ambiguity, which would reinforce the charm (etymologically speaking) of the stranger. Dominique searched for a long time. Suddenly he had an illumination: but surely! The name shared by the two women followed by a question mark would perfectly serve the purpose: *Patricia?*

The writer was convinced that one could love only once in a lifetime: that would be the single authentic love. After him, those "other times" were but replicas without savor, pallid copies and nothing else. Every time he set out this "theory" based on his own experience, he would find an earnest objector. Generally, the writer wouldn't insist on the subject. What did Reverdy mean by his *showing of love?* And

Laetitia, whom he never questioned? And...Nora? Or finally his daughters? They always kept very secretive about their love lives, but perhaps Laetitia had benefited from their trust? Laure seemed to him the most vulnerable of the two, maybe more secretive apparently. Dominique was eager for them to discover the greatest of loves, the one love for which a whole lifetime couldn't suffice. That mad *amour that* would allow the lovers to forget *the devastation of the world....* He remembered the end of a letter Andre Breton wrote to his daughter Aube: "My wish for you is that somebody will love you madly." Oh, yes, thought Dominique: "To be *madly loved* and love madly too. Nothing else." He would have loved to be able to say this to Natacha and Laure, although he knew very well that he wouldn't allow himself to say any such thing; they would probably be shocked by their father's lack of decorum. "Who does he think he is telling us what to do?" they would certainly think. Melancholy invaded Dominique, typically of his Russian side, as Laetitia would put it.

*

He was suddenly interrupted by his wife, who asked him, "What's up? Is that manuscript advancing?" He nodded. She observed him closely and for a long time.

"I am under the impression that your getaway to Hungary did you good. All is for the better then."

Her husband didn't answer. This silence disconcerted Laetitia. Usually he would be very anxious to solicit her advice regarding his work, looking for signs of approval and suggestions, which she would gladly give him. This obstinate silence wasn't like the man she thought she knew through and through. Laetitia was hurt. He sensed this.

She seemed to think about it and then added, "You are right; we could go for a little spin at Pecs. Easter holidays are approaching. What do you think? Her husband had a contrary feeling. He didn't want to share Pecs with Laetitia any longer. But how could he confess it? It was out of the question.

"Why not....We'll talk about it again," he answered shortly. "I may be giving some conferences there at the University anyhow."

Then he changed the subject.

"Listen, one day I would like to prepare a Hungarian dish, a fish soup typically from Pecs, a halászlé[†], but we will have to find carp. There are also other kinds of fish, I think."

Laetitia pouted.

"I don't think carp is a particularly tasty fish. It has a lot of bones....Anyhow, why not?"

"I'll take them out for you! In any case I don't remember finding the least bone when I ate this very tasty soup with Nora at Blöff Bisztro ‡.... Why couldn't we give it a try?"

4

William Cole announced to him that one of his books would probably be chosen the following year at Benson College for the B.A. in Language and French literature, at the suggestion of the students in accordance with their French professor. The American asked if he had any preferences. Dominique responded that he was honored by the selection; he'd think about it and would let him know soon.... The professor mentioned also the possibility of co-organizing some writing workshops for the next year and maybe even for the years following.

"*My dear, you've caused a commotion at Benson College!*" [6] Cole wrote to him, amid other compliments.

*

The writer confirmed to his editor that the manuscript was on its way, without giving him too many details about the finish. It seemed that Macor was always very comprehensive regarding the writer: he simply wished him lots of luck, thanking him profusely.

---

[6]   In English in the original.

5

The couple lived in an old stone house that once belonged to Dominique's maternal grandparents, in Fargette, a small village of Essonne not far from Milly-La-Forêt. Laetitia was very much attached to their nest, as she called it. Her husband confessed to her once that he couldn't live in the house all by himself because there were so many souvenirs of his childhood linked to this much loved place. Despite its proximity of the capital, the calm village suited their life perfectly. Dominique liked to do what he called a pilgrimage to Saint-Blaise des Simples's chapel, where Jean Cocteau was buried. As a child, he visited this tomb with his parents. It was a family ritual of sorts that the little boy appreciated very much. He stayed for a long time in front of Cocteau's estate, day-dreaming, imagining it as being the castle of the Beast. He would close his eyes, seeing a smiling Jean Cocteau hurrying toward him, welcoming him into his house. In his soul, little Dominique knew precisely that this event wouldn't ever happen because the writer had died a few years back, but the inscription *I'll stay with you,* etched into the chapel's floor, was a proof to the contrary, a transcendental manifestation.

Dominique Valarcher felt at peace, in accordance with his own self, for one of the rarest times of his life. He was under the impression that he had arrived at a superior level in his writing career. New perspectives were opening up in front of his eyes. He was yet young and at the cross-roads. The writer rubbed his hands. He would dedicate his latest manuscript to Nora, in remembrance of Pecs. Never in his life had Dominique felt so good, so much in harmony and this serenity was due at least in part to the young girl. A writer is a spoiled and selfish child who needs to be loved, understood and surely encouraged nonstop. Valarcher wouldn't escape this rule. Wanting to be alone and to write, this ascetic life, was irrefutable proof of a form of neurosis. A writer knows this better than anyone, but at times he indulged himself with this passion exorbitantly. Dominique Valarcher remembered how a scathing review of his first book had wounded him: it wasn't possible! "They" didn't like his novel; "they" demolished it with relish. Who gave them the right? On whose account? Who dared commit a crime of Lese-majeste like that? Laetitia did her best to reassure him about his talent: "My husband is a great writer.

The reviewers are donkey idiots who wouldn't know better." That day, he had the urge to break everything in his study, destroy all his unfinished manuscripts, and also his books. His wife had been hard pressed to hold him back and reassure him. All at once Dominique changed into a purple-faced child whose favorite toy "they" had broken. That outrage was by now a thing of the past, but he kept the painful memory and a rancour that had kept him from writing again for some months.... He also consulted a psychiatrist who affirmed that one had to accept remaining a child in certain matters, that this revolt would give him the means to continue his work as a writer, and even to nourish his work somehow. He was right: whatever the psychiatrist predicted happened. His second book, *The Falsification of Nothing*, a poetry collection, constituted a kind of therapy, even if it didn't bring about lots of success. His editor accepted it immediately with no problems. Dominique was reassured, justified and understood, like a spoiled child. Afterwards, the relationship with that particular editor deteriorated. He often reproached the writer that his poetry collections couldn't get off the ground as far as sales, which irritated Dominique. He violently accused the editor of doing nothing to ensure the promotion of his work, which was justified. The tone of the discussion rose. Naturally each of them maintained their position. The following book, a novel, sold well. The recriminations stopped altogether. Nevertheless Dominique remained annoyed with the editor for a long time, just for his brutality.

*

Dominique had regained his inner balance, which was essential for his creativity. He was translated soon into Romanian, Greek and English in the United States. At times his books sold better outside the country. He conceived a curious pride reasoning that the fact that he was better appreciated and studied in Romanian and American Universities proved yet again the mediocrity of a certain French critique that he tried hard to erase from his mind. "*No one is a prophet in his own country,*" he often repeated. Maybe he wasn't that wrong....

Apparently that's the way the world goes. The microcosm of a writer is sometimes (often) very small and smooth, closed in on itself like a beautiful useless object. If the world didn't understand his voice, well, it didn't matter! The world is stupid or simply deaf. Valarcher was aware of this pretention when...he wasn't writing! It is true that the majority of his "colleagues" — poets in particular — persuaded themselves that they were geniuses... poorly understood, that went without saying. A certain nobody did publish two poems in a secret magazine, and he remained thank God a nobody, but he considered himself the greatest! One could be listening to his perorations about his Art at every Paris literary workshop. Dominique had stopped frequenting those places where the spirit can't breathe. Worse, he would run away from such places, provoking the desperation of his editors who considered that the author should show himself in public, give his opinion on everything, go to have cocktails.... In short, be widely seen and if possible accompanied by influential people, surrounded by young gorgeous women with crystalline laughter, a glass of champagne in his hand. When he was younger, influenced by some acquaintances, the writer went along with this whirlwind, but fortunately he got out of it without too much damage. Laetitia would never accompany him.

"Why lose one's time frequenting these superficial soirees Paris is known for, which have nothing to do with literature?" she would decry with disdain.

Dominique had to admit that she was right.

*

"Writing is a solitary endeavor and that's the way it has to be; otherwise, it is only posturing," he burst out during a Radio interview. They had asked him to be more precise in his assertion. He changed the subject, claiming he didn't have to justify himself. The reporter didn't insist and instead asked why according to him none of the literary shows on TV treated the subject of poetry. He answered curtly that it was because "the middle-classes read or pretend to read novels and then why waste one's time with a literary genre meant for *some select few,* a genre that doesn't interest anybody, least of all the ignorant hosts of the so called cultural programs."

After, he regretted that outburst, which, sound as it was, didn't shed any light on the debate. One of his colleagues drew his attention to the fact that he risked becoming a *persona non grata* in the eyes of French TV and that a writer should stay "*consensual*" but for Dominique there was no hope. Moreover he judged that the opinion of that particular colleague was without doubt exaggerated. Future experiences proved to him that he was right.

Nobody took his biting words seriously. The literary Republic didn't crumble as a result of this storm in a teacup.

That night Laetitia confessed that she really appreciated his sincerity—or brutality?—for answering like that, without mentioning the rest of the program. Her husband, who was after all a sentimental man, replied simply, "I love you." Everything was said and they opened a bottle of champagne which they drank, lovey-dovey. When Laetitia undressed slowly to prolong his pleasure, Dominique closed his eyes halfway, savoring the privileged moment.

*

Dominique Valarcher received news from Nora. The student wrote that her Masters was advancing little by little. Unfortunately she wouldn't be able to visit him in France, she didn't have the money. He lamented this, reassuring her that they would find a way to meet. He made a promise to himself to talk to Laetitia about a possible week in Pecs so he could take advantage of the trip and take some documents to Nora.

6

Around 10 years prior, Laetitia left the house for three days without telling anybody. She simply didn't come back from work. She took nothing with her. Not a suitcase, or toiletry bag, not even her cellphone. Dominique was very worried. Laetitia wasn't one to fantasize. She disappeared without apparent reason; they hadn't fought. After hesitating for a long time, he decided not to call the police. His intuition told him that his wife hadn't been kidnapped or had an accident. He felt that she had acted on her own will without being able to understand why. He was left prostrated, locked in his house, the shutters closed, content to feed the cat that kept its cool.

*

When Laetitia returned, she found her husband crying in front of his turned-down computer. He watched her with a distracted eye without recognizing her and speaking incoherently. Some ripped off blank papers were spread around on the floor. She didn't dare to look at him. She just mumbled, "Nothing ever happens to us. Our life is so dull."

Dominique didn't ask her for explanations. He didn't have the strength. With his wife's leaving, he lost one of his reasons to live. Without Laetitia nothing existed anymore. Not even writing.

That night they drank a lot, although that never happened to them before. At dessert, she took her husband by the hand and made him sit on the sofa in the salon.

"Make yourself comfortable. The show will start soon," she whispered into his ear.

The lights slowly dimmed, something unusual was about to happen, Dominique's heart was pounding in his chest. She put on a CD of *The Prelude to the Afternoon of a Faun* by Debussy, a piece that her husband liked very much. Frozen, making himself as discreet as possible, holding his hands on his knees, he was contemplating her without saying a word. Laetitia kept still for a moment, facing him, and suddenly his wife's body started shaking imperceptibly. She began to caress her breasts through her blue-marine dress, making indecent gestures, and then swayed her hips more and more frenetically. Dominique had never seen his wife like this. It was probably due to the excess of alcohol, as in a trance. Fascinated, he couldn't take his eyes off this barbaric deity who was offering herself in this way to him. Dominique hardly recognized Laetitia in that indecent creature, her rump extended toward his manliness and who excited his senses by the way she caressed herself more and more. She started moaning and undressed progressively in front of her husband, who was very aroused by this spectacle. The lights became dimmer still.... When she appeared in a black thong, dancing closer and closer, he simply couldn't resist anymore; the moment she touched him, dangerously undulating her body provocatively, he jumped on a consenting Laetitia, who was waiting for this assault, and he took her breasts in his hands. Both crashed on the floor. The woman who offered herself this way was completely metamorphosed. He had never seen her like that, panting with difficulty and with her eyes illuminated by a strange light, almost unreal. The show ended up on the carpet and with the great satisfaction of the couple in heat. Never before had they made love with so much savageness. Their desire for each other was raw and their complicity perfect.

Out of breath, the writer managed to say, "Will you repeat this? I adored your show! I'll pay to 'see it again!"

Instead of answering, his wife jumped on him and pinned him on the floor, straddling him with ardor.

*

They never mentioned that evening again, at least not overtly.

"We understand each other with half-words," his wife often affirmed. The enactment of that unusual scene amply upheld this.

*

What did happen during Laetitia's absence? Where did she go? What did she do? Her husband didn't want to know, or, at least, he didn't believe he was authorized to interrogate his wife on the subject. He had been amply compensated for his anguish during those three days that seemed like an eternity to him.

Sometime after, Dominique risked to question her.

"Do you think that we could let ourselves go this evening?" he asked with a suggestive wink. But it was in vain because they never regained the magic of that intimate show, accentuated without doubt by frustration. Dominique would have liked to prolong that experience by writing an erotic short story but he wasn't able to do so. He didn't formalize by lack of success. He wondered what his wife would think of reading the short story in question. He didn't regret anything. Yet who could say? Must a writer at any cost reproduce certain intimate situations through literature? Better not put the question to her, he thought.

That's the way of the world....

*

"*[T]he world is forever tossing. All things jerk off with no letup,*" affirmed Montaigne. [7]

Dominique Valarcher remembered the hilarity of some foolish boys when listening to this citation mentioned by their philosophy professor, in their senior year class. For sure he would never be on the side of these pitiful victims of a prudish education, he thought despising them at that time. [8]

"Montaigne... such a free spirit, this

---

[7] English translation by Charles Cotton. Edited by William Carew Hazlitt (1877).

[8] The school kids are laughing because in Montaigne's 16th Century French the words he uses "branloire" and "branle" in modern French have taken on the sense of "to masturbate."

Montaigne, without prejudice and so very French! I adore savoring a page of his essays like a tonic or a good wine," said a young professor at Benson College with a vague smile on his face. This confidence moved the writer who answered maliciously.

"A tonic or a good drink of wine, isn't that the same?"

*

This evening he thought of Laetitia's escapade, which set up the unexpected show performed by his wife.

"Nothing ever happens to us. Our life is so dull." This sentence went round and around in his head like a sort of reproach. What had she meant to say? Did Laetitia think it was the same now? Dominique promised himself to ask her about it, seriously. He needed certainties. But even so, he knew that he wouldn't do it, in remembrance of that wild night when sex had replaced feelings for a while.

The couple decided to spend a week in Pecs, at the end of May. Maybe they would be able to rent the apartment on Ifusag Street. Dominique would look into this.

When Laetitia and Dominique arrived in Pecs, the weather was very mild, as when the writer visited the place for the first time. This time Nora welcomed them at the airport. Dominique felt a sharp pang in his heart when he saw her from the distance. He suddenly understood how much he missed her. She waved at the couple and rushed toward them.

"Welcome to Hungary!" she exclaimed, smiling. "It's so kind of you to come here together!"

Then turning around to Laetitia, "I am so pleased to meet you!"

"Me too! Dominique has spoken with such enthusiasm about Pecs, so it wasn't hard to convince me!" she answered.

The taxi dropped them off in front of the apartment building. Dominique told Nora that he had some work to do at the Library.

"If you like, we could meet later on this afternoon at the Paulus café. We'll talk about your projects."

After leaving their bags, the couple decided to go immediately to see the cathedral Saint-Pierre.

"I'm so happy to be here with you," whispered

Laetitia caressing his hand. Yes, decidedly, the last piece of the puzzle will have to wait. Pecs was the city of lovers, Dominique was absolutely convinced.

.*

Exactly like her husband, Laetitia fell for the charm of Pecs. In a low voice she started reciting *Allegiance* by Rene Char: "*Here is my love, on the streets of the city. He could go anywhere in these troubled times. He is no longer my lover; anyone can speak with him....*"

She seemed so very happy, hanging on her companion's arm! He thought that one day death would separate them. It would be necessary for the other to be able to find in common memories the courage to continue to live or the urge to succumb. Sometimes he found himself in turmoil of contradictory feelings that forbade him to appreciate the present moment.

Dominique had always had a problem letting go, without understanding why very well. Laetitia often repeated that her husband asked himself too many questions. She was convinced that happiness was much simpler than it appeared, that it was sufficient simply to believe. In her opinion it was useless to regret the past. Decisions, bad or good, had been taken once and for all. After that you had to go on to another thing. Exactly on this point the couple never could come to an agreement. Dominique would say nobody could be exonerated from the past, which would weigh with all its might on the life of humans; he was thinking especially of the family secret he discovered as a child, and that he quietly revealed to Laetitia. The ghosts of his mother became his ghosts because he wasn't able to impart this discovery to Camille Valarcher, the woman who gave him life. There wasn't anything worse than self-censorship, Dominique thought, without possessing the power to turn from this reality. His mother's cross became his cross. In any case now it was too late. No analysis would deliver him from the terrible truth he'd learned from the mouth of Camille *who her first husband was.* His mother was now dead; his father too. The love words of this Paul Barbier, the happy chosen one, everything, even his name, had made Dominique an heir of the writer, a victim of this passionate drama, of a true tragedy that should have remained the property of his mother, exclusively. Camille Valarcher, the widow of Barbier, would have liked to have a daughter, named Dominique, with Louis Valarcher for honoring the memory of another man, an intruder, almost an impostor in the writer's eye. That girl would have been his reincarnation. All was so simple apparently: the young woman had but a single love, the first, him, *the other*, the Prince Charming from the fairy tales. Dominique's father would remain forever the eternal second, a double. That idealized first love excluded Louis Valarcher, made a pale copy of him, the exact opposite of the original that his mother had lost at the age of twenty-two without ever finding solace, Dominique was convinced.

How could she imagine that her son would discover the painful secret that she never dared unveil? *Never wanted to unveil it?* Nevertheless the son couldn't be angry with his mother for preserving in her intimacy like this.

*

Dominique, *the divided, the fractured, the romantic...* he would have loved to open his heart in front of Nora, to share it all with her. He felt that these revelations would draw them nearer but understood that he couldn't free himself from such a burden. How would the young girl react? After all, the student was working on his fiction and not on his psyche. Anyhow...could these things be dissociated? Thinking about it he understood that nothing could justify such an egotistic attitude on his part. No, he would keep Nora away from his neurosis. He respected her too much.

*

The following day, leaving Laetitia to explore Pecs by herself, Dominique met with Nora at the usual Coffee-house, a little more tranquil than usual. He gave her some books and other personal documents, particularly *Patricia?* his last novel. He wasn't anxious at this moment to rejoin his wife. The young girl suggested they go to her apartment, which he gladly accepted. Nora lived in a duplex with a mansard in the historic town center. The writer reiterated how much Laetitia and he would love for her to come and stay with them in France, when she could travel. The student thanked him, smiling; she really was the living portrait of Tatiana Samoilova....He was emotional, even troubled in her presence, unable to put his finger on what was troubling him. Suddenly Nora jumped into his arms. They embraced one another for a swollen moment. Dominique had the urge to bury his head in the long and thick hair of the girl. She smelled like *Diorella*, the perfume Laure used. Diorella...the perfume he offered her the first time they met. In this respect, *he wanted this moment to last forever*. Nora kept still, not moving at all. Finally she raised her head, with tears in her eyes.

"I beg your pardon," she mumbled blushing. "You must think that I'm bold....But it is the word that is feeble...."

"No," he answered. "You are a warm and straightforward young girl. In French we say *une fleur bleue*. You are spontaneous. Don't be afraid, I loved this moment we shared. How do you say this...I think I consider you a little as my own daughter, excuse me ...Thank you for confiding in me...."

She smiled.

"Thanks. Laetitia is so beautiful. It's good to see how in love you are.... You seem so very...so close, both of you."

"I've often been told that. We've been together for a long time, a very long time, ever since college, in fact.... Almost," he sighed "for eternity...."

"I didn't know this expression, *blue flower*...I like it a lot. I think that..." She hesitated. "I think that you're a blue flower also, Dominique."

The writer smiled back to her. He felt understood. Their sensibilities were totally in tune. As in a painting by Chagall, an angel passed high above them. He skimmed the peaceful sky of Pecs then disappeared. Nora and Dominique didn't notice. The trace vanished progressively. Perhaps nothing happened at all.

Dominique Valarcher was happy, at peace. He vowed to learn a few words in Hungarian, if anything only to be polite. Decidedly, death had to wait....

*

In high school one of his girl friends told him with a complicit smile, "Dominique, you are an incurable romantic!"

"Already"...thought the writer.

He simply confessed to Nora that he felt happy. Would she accept working with him on a book of essays? He would talk to Macor about it. The student agreed. Brusquely, without thinking, the writer took refuge in her arms. His heart was pounding. Nora reassured him. He had never in his life felt such serenity.

"Not even with Laetitia?" whispered a small interior voice in a harsh tone. The writer preferred to ignore it.

Dominique contemplated writing a short story, *The Fairy of Pecs.* For once there would be a happy ending. He would dedicate it to Nora.

Night was falling. They went out to join

Laetitia. Arm in arm the three of them started looking for a restaurant. That evening after drinking a few bottles of bikavér* wine with their plates of lecsó[†], they left the restaurant very late and in a drunken state. They staggered a little, holding onto one another with grand bursts of laughter leaning on the walls in order to keep their balance. Dominique now held Nora, now Laetitia in his arms. Neither of them objected. The pair managed to accompany Nora back to her apartment and reached theirs without incident.

*

The next day Dominique received a text from Nora:

"I have a little headache this morning but it was a delicious evening:

Köszönöm, barátaim. Mindig szívemben éltek majd." [‡]

8

Going back to France was hard for the pair. That city Pecs was without doubt magnificent. They felt empty. Everything went so fast, much too fast, as if at any cost they had to recapture their lost years, in a very little time. Laetitia and Dominique were sobering up in all the senses of the term. Nora cried when she accompanied them to the airport. She fell into their arms. Laetitia promised her that they would see each other again. They vowed enduring friendship. On their arrival in France it was raining. Pecs was far away. Laetitia and Dominique looked at each other sadly without uttering a word.

The same evening they listened to *The Prelude to the Afternoon of a Faun* When the first notes started playing they looked at one another, each smiling eloquently but the magic wasn't there, they had to admit. Tired, they went to bed early and that was that.

*

Dominique was very happy that Nora and his wife got along so well. The evening at the restaurant sealed an enduring friendship between them. Dominique was content.

Jean-Francois Macor readily consented to a

book of interviews, after the short stories came out. "There's nothing pressing us," he said, using his favorite expression. "Take your time." And the leitmotif was repeated again and again. For the first time the writer had a smooth rapport with a French editor. This seldom happened! He hurried to announce the good news to Nora. It was all the more important and urgent for her now to finish her Master's. After that, they would see....

Laetitia slept late that morning. She didn't have classes. Dominique woke up early. He had a hard time getting started with his work. His mind was in another place. All day he thought of Nora. The garden was in bloom. So was his heart. While the writer meandered in this way on the garden's alleyways, a bird flapped off and startled him. He didn't feel like doing anything, sit in the shade of an apple tree, on the old bench painted green and flaked, take his time to daydream or distractedly leaf through a book.

Finally he sat down some minutes before going inside. Let's agree to it, life is beautiful and love eternal! At the same time, this adage wasn't enough to dissipate his recurring melancholy.

That day, his manuscript didn't advance much,

but even this inactivity left him indifferent. He would have wanted to stay in Pecs with Nora. Nothing else.

Laetitia smiled at him from afar. She was rereading an anthology of Russian poetry by Katia Granoff, and was taking some notes. She bought the book in a bookstore in the Latin Quarter when they were students. The shop—as they called it—was replaced by a McDonald's some time ago.

In the introduction, as a corroboration, the translator affirmed that Russian poetry had been written "with the blood of the poets." Was this the reason the literature of this tragic country is one of the most beautiful in the world? Louis Valarcher thought so. His son approved without reservations.

Not too far from the Sorbonne, Michka, a small Russian restaurant kept by a family who called them affectionately "the lovers," had disappeared also. Curiously, Dominique felt no bitterness about it. The banks and the second-hand boutiques proliferated and replaced the bookstores as was the case everywhere else. One day perhaps they will perish altogether. At times Dominique felt he was very old but Laetitia was always at his side...for how much time? How many books would he manage to write from now on and why? He was dreaming of a world which would eclipse the banks where the spirit flourished, the souvenir boutiques *made in China*...Who knows? But he would be dead by then, he was sure.

Laetitia was watching him. Their looks crossed. How beautiful she was! What was his wife thinking at this very moment? Dominique lowered his eyes. He was wondering if his wife was nostalgic for *Michka*, for their young years, for the *fleur bleue* student who professed his love for her through the intermediary of a poem, for their developing relation.... It wouldn't do any good to be sentimental, to feel pity for a past supposedly idyllic, since anyhow death would sweep it all away in the end, but as she well knew, her husband wasn't able to stop himself.

*

Death.... How was Camille able to surpass the disappearance of her first love? Married at twenty, a widow at twenty-two.... And she must have had to survive in order to try to live.... How could she do it? Dominique dwelt on the same questions, over and over.

All these questions without answers were killing Dominique. His childhood broke down at twelve years of age, somehow. He would have liked to forget about that revelation. It haunted him constantly, it was the filigree of his writing, he was conscious about it. It was a stigmata that couldn't be erased, a wound that would open again and again...

*

Suddenly he thought that his enchantment for *The Prelude to the Afternoon of a Faun* had perhaps disappeared. He didn't dare ask Laetitia her opinion about this matter. Perhaps the magic of an evening brought about by an excess of emotions would never resurrect again.

Yet Nora filled his thoughts. She wholly intrigued both the writer and the man. He would have to talk with Laetitia. Dominique also wondered how "the famous" evening at the restaurant in Pecs had started. It was true the three of them were so happy together! Nora was very seductive that evening, her eyes were shining and her accent was really delicious! The writer would have wanted to unburden his heart. The girl would have blushed probably under the benevolent glance of Laetitia. Dominique remembered all this with emotion: he spied more or less on Nora with her complicity, lying in wait for her reactions. Her laughter made him happy. Dominique envied this joie de vivre, this freshness which was ever took him by surprise. Sometimes their looks crossed.

The student resembled Tatiana Samoilova more than ever.

Dominique couldn't have understood it better. Nora perfectly symbolized the reincarnation theory in which he never believed and which hit him so very hard ruining his certitudes.

Dominique Valarcher didn't write this day. He was incapable of it. He didn't want to feel any regrets. Tomorrow would be another day, as the old saying goes.

All at once, a few piano chords drew him from his reveries. Laetitia? His wife had once practiced this instrument. Then, they had bought a piano for Natasha who also played it for a few years and just stopped as an adolescent, proclaiming that she was no good at it. Laure in her turn was never interested in music. But Laetitia? Such a long time had gone by.... Dominique recognized this Ravel piece that he particularly liked. He kept at a distance not wanting to disturb her. His wife was far off, in another world where her husband didn't have access, and he suddenly envied her for bringing these sounds that took them back years to life from the instrument. Suddenly the piano fell silent. She sensed his presence and now was looking at him. Laetitia was very pallid.

"What an idea...I shouldn't have...," she whispered. He thought he'd seen tears in her eyes. Dominique would have liked to regain, even for an instant, the young girl who seduced him when he was a student. For the length of a poem, he would have traced the contour of their hands joined on the sky, thanking the one he loved so much, here and now

*

"Was it *Jeux d'eau* ?" he asked. She nodded. Laetitia seemed to regret that moment of abandonment. He stopped himself from complimenting her, knowing too well that she would be embarrassed by any lavishment. A long time ago he asked her why she stopped playing. Laetitia talked about the class work she had, the copies to correct, but he knew perfectly well that she wasn't telling the truth. Nevertheless, this day....

In that instant he realized how dear his wife was to him. It was difficult to explain but he loved her *also* for those piano notes that were about to spring forth from her fingers. He suddenly understood that Nora reminded him of Laetitia in her youth, of her beauty, her intelligence, even if the two were totally different. Dominique didn't know how to express what he was feeling. He was submerged by a sensation that literally choked literary. Everything toppled over. Everything was confusing. *An incurable romantic....* Decidedly, the same expressions had accompanied him all his life. There was no escape.

Dominique decided to keep his thoughts to himself. Laetitia closed the piano's lid with a sharp bang, and quickly left the room without looking back. The writer felt all at once the need to cry. He should have rushed after his wife to console her. A coward, he was feeling worthless like the heroes of his books: all these men who could only abdicate, run away from their responsibilities.

9

The next day Dominique woke up late. Laetitia was already gone. He found a piece of paper on the kitchen table. Scribbled on it in capital letters were these simple words: I LOVE YOU. He felt ashamed without knowing why. He would always be a little fragile boy. Maybe it was time to grow up and be a man, forgetting Eastern Europe, and the death of Paul Barbier at Auschwitz, going on with his life without looking back.

*

Dominique could again see himself in Nora's arms. It became a real obsession by now. He would have liked to turn back to Pecs and walk the streets with the young girl arm in arm and nothing else. The writer would offer her *Diorella*, she would jump into his arms smiling, like the first time in her apartment. "How easy everything was!" he thought bitterly. His mind was wandering.... Laetitia was playing the piano, Nora at their side, her hand on Dominique's shoulder, watching them. The writer sighed. He wondered once more what it was that kept him in front of the computer's screen for hours and hours. The day he'd be able to answer this would be the day he'd put an end to his work, he was certain. That would be a death stop; he wouldn't be able to write again, because literature dies of too many justifications.

How many times they asked him the eternal question, "Why do you write?"

Dominique knew the immutable answer: "To forget about death. Meaning, I write in vain."

Every time, though, he eluded the question: "The real question is 'for whom?' and not 'What for?' The truth is I don't know."

*

The telephone rang. Jean-Francois Macor proposed that he make a presentation of his upcoming book in Paris in a few weeks. Maybe he could read some new texts? Dominique agreed to it all; yes, he'd be there. Yes, that would be lovely. Yes, he'd read one or two short stories. Yes, yes, yes, for sure.... After he hung up he regretted accepting this proposition.

"How simple everything was!" he thought again. But overall, what was happening? Dominique had obtained whatever he had desired for such a long time: financial freedom. He was known in France and more outside the country; people were writing articles, essays on his books; his books were studied in the program of one of the most prestigious American universities; in Alba Iulia, in Athens, professors were teaching classes on his latest poetry collections; he was even asked to give conferences, present manuscripts.... What more did he need? No, nothing was so simple really.

The writer didn't understand what was happening with him. If he could he would jump on the first plane destined for Pecs. He didn't recognize himself anymore. What was happening with Nora?

*

Why did it take Dominique so long to put two and two together? He was in love with that student, as simply as that. How was it possible? It felt like he was caught in a trap. But what trap? And who caught him in it? It couldn't have been Nora.

Someone would be amazed by, or would mock the candor of a man 50 years of age like Dominique Valarcher.

"My God, am I in love with another woman? How is this possible, how did it happen to me, Dominique Valarcher, the man of eternal faith?"

But this would amount to not really knowing, not the man or the writer.

He reproached himself for his lack of foresight.

And that word was weak.

We know Oscar Wilde's assertion *"Faithfulness is to the emotional life what consistency is to the life of the intellect—simply a confession of failure."* Nothing was so foreign to Valarcher for whom life, his life, was summed up by his long love story that joined him to Laetitia. The man who in the past was living *on the balcony of stars,* this man didn't understand the new situation; his sincerity could not be put in doubt. He was defeated, worse he was devastated. Yes, Dominique fell into a trap and knew that he was responsible. What to do now? Confess to Laetitia? Stop seeing Nora? But, how to do it? Under what pretense? The best would probably be to fly to Hungary and say good bye to the girl....

"Would that really be the best thing? How simple!—How hypocritical!" the small interior voice, ever bitter, ventured. Dominique preferred to ignore it, as he had the first time.

10

By the day of the conference, the writer had resolved his sentimental problem. How on earth could someone love two beings as different as Laetitia and Nora? He was under the impression that his wife understood what was going on with him. She watched him covertly at times, but he pretended not to notice. Was he capable of cheating on the woman of his life and at the same time hurting Nora? What was he to do?

At other times, he tried to convince himself that playing an ambiguous role wasn't that disagreeable after all. Nora was intelligent, seducing; she admired the writer and appreciated the man. Nevertheless, it was she who gave into spontaneity, threw herself into his arms..... But, this "justification" wasn't the right one; Valarcher was fully aware of it. He was mad with himself for so much hypocrisy. He didn't know what else to think....

*

Jean-François Macor welcomed him with a big smile.

"Good day Dominique. I am so pleased by your acceptance of my suggestion." People started arriving. "Surely the name of Dominique Valarcher draws a lot of people. There are even foreigners. You can hear English being spoken, and Italian, as well as languages from the East that I don't understand. Come over, please."

Dominique obliged. Macor was affable, courteous. The writer wasn't used to being so pampered by his usual French editor and that was a euphemism! In other circumstances he would have answered favorably to these advances. He made an effort to cheer up, if only by politeness, thanking the editor.

The place was at elbow room. Dominique Valarcher managed to forget his apprehensions for the moment. Relaxed, Jean-Francois Macor made a brief introduction of the writer and his themes before inviting him speak. Dominique read two short stories, took a pause and then asked the audience for questions. Little by little the debate started.

Answering the question "What's the writer's responsibility toward the world?" Dominique positioned himself on the side of Camus, whom he discovered as an adolescent. He cited *The Sweden Discourse*, where his favorite author reminded the audience that the writer must put himself at the service of those who endured history, even if this engagement as noble as it is would never rid the artist of his solitude.

A reader wondered why she didn't see in his work any allusion to the big problems of society, or to the fate of the miserable people of the world. He answered that there weren't any contradictions in this, that engagement concerned him more as the citizen Valarcher than the writer Valarcher. He relaxed little by little and regained his confidence. He was in his element. A woman dressed in a blue suit, seated in the third row, would not take her eyes off of him. The writer thought that she resembled Laetitia. Dominique half-smiled at her, and she did the same. Obviously she was feverishly taking notes. It was the turn of an adolescent girl who wanted to know if by writing one was living by procuration. The writer thought a second before answering.

"Yes, definitely. While playing the role of a Demiurge giving life to paper heroes, one forgets about the real world. This is a splitting in two of sorts that could end up by being dangerous after a while. The writer is an egoist; he isolates himself, abandoning himself to his favorite occupation while the world continues as ever with its injustices and tragedies, while people suffer and die.... These attitudes are immoral."

Then a middle-aged man with a thick accent asked why Eastern Europe was so prominent in his books. Dominique affirmed that his father was of distant Russian origins and that he himself had always been fascinated by the art and culture of oriental Europe. In his opinion Russian and Soviet literature—and notably the poetry—was one of the most beautiful of the world.

"Tragedy is inscribed for eternity into the history of this vast country that never knew democracy as Poland, Czechoslovakia, and Hungary at various levels...." He hesitated. "The list is limitless," he mumbled again, his voice trembling with emotion.

"Death comes from the East," he added. His altered voice broke suddenly. A young woman rose, stretched her arms in his direction, as though to embrace him. She uttered some words that he didn't understand. There were a few applauses coming mostly from the back of the room. They passed a note along to him on which was written in red letters "Thank you. **Ты наш!**"*

When he made a nod in the direction where

the applause came from, the writer seemed suddenly very tired. He would have liked to run away forever, far, very far to sigh out his chagrin on unknown shores. Impossible though, the world would catch up with him and take him by the throat.

*

During the pause, as everyone was taking refreshments and savoring finger food, the woman from the third row approached him. She was Italian, working for a Press and wished to translate his future short story collection and maybe a play into Italian. Up front her resemblance to Laetitia wasn't so apparent anymore. Dominique was relieved without understanding clearly why. Jean-Francois Macor approached him. Evidently, he was satisfied.

"We have to find a title for our book, Dominique," he remarked. "Madame Carlotta Bonini," he turned over toward the Italian woman and nodded gallantly, "whom you already met, represents the *Alla Lettera Press* from Italy. She's going to put us in contact with their director. We'll talk again next week, you and I, at your convenience." Valarcher nodded. Macor was satisfied. What could be more natural? The writer started to appreciate this cultivated man who always showed respect for his work and for the time put into his writing. "Carlotta proposed that we meet in Rome in a few months to encounter the editor Mr. Giovanni Mogherini."

Dominique Valarcher answered a few more questions, notably one from an old woman on his concept of love, which embarrassed him a lot. In a few lyrical phrases he resumed—without naming Laetitia—his sentiments towards the loved one giving a vibrant praise for the fidelity that marked a man as a chosen being and allowed his ascension to a superior dimension, then thanked the audience. They applauded him for a long time. Carlotta waved at him from a distance then left pointing to her watch. Apparently she was in a hurry. He could now see no resemblance between her and Laetitia, even from afar, and that made him happy.

11

That evening it felt good to Dominique to get back to their house in Fargette. More than ever he needed solitude and conjugal tenderness. Laetitia was waiting for him. When she looked at him, he turned his eyes away. She threw herself into his arms burying her head in his chest. Dominique was in love with her, he was certain. He knew his wife could read his thoughts. He held her in his arms for a long while. He wouldn't dare ask her to sit at the piano. He would have liked to hear something by Debussy, maybe *Suite Bergamasque* that he loved dearly and that he associated rightly with Verlaine, one of his favorite poets. Finally Dominique made the request. His voice was shaky. Against all hope, Laetitia agreed. He would have liked to die there, quietly, listening to her play the piano. He wondered one more time why he would associate happiness with death, exclusively his own. The remaining of the evening was quiet. He uncorked a bottle of Saumur Champigny, one of his wife's favorite wines. She drank a few sips between the pieces. Suddenly, when the pianist rose to change the score, he leaned over her, slowly but firmly unbuttoned her corsage, undid her bra. Laetitia didn't protest, she sat back at the piano and continued playing, her breasts naked as if nothing had happened. Dominique dimmed the lights. At times, Laetitia's bosom started following the higher rhythm of a piece. At 50, her breasts, which many younger women could have envied, stood round and firm.

He made himself as discreet as possible so the interpreter would be free to forget about his presence. Dominique had an idea: Why not write a short story inspired by that moment of intimacy, a story about a piano player with bare breasts who was wandering the world from concert to concert enchanting— overwhelming the music lovers? The writer wondered if this idea was an original one. It mustn't be at any cost a cheap erotic thing. He imagined Laetitia with her torso naked, playing Debussy, Ravel, Poulenc and Fauré facing a stunned audience. All of the women in the theater at each performance would do the same, exhibiting their breasts together. It would be a ritual of sorts that would be transmitted everywhere on the planet. Laetitia finished. She turned towards him making as though to put on her blouse. He shook his head and nodded toward the piano. She made a curious face and played a few minutes more. He seemed to recognize Chopin's *Nocturne.*

How much time had this privileged concert lasted? He didn't care. It was without doubt late. Fascinated, the writer wished to remain like this watching Laetitia, his accomplice who played naked just for him. All of the sudden they were in darkness. Who had turned off the lights? There wasn't any noise. When the pianist approached him, he opened his arms and squeezed her against him. She took the hands of her husband and placed them on her breasts, hung onto him and moaned.... Nothing else had any importance...his obsession with death faded.... His interior voice stopped harassing him.

*

Laetitia's serenade was reserved exclusively for Dominique, and yet it troubled him. Both of them liked Debussy very much. His wife was an excellent interpreter. When she was younger she thought of studying to pursue a musical career and become a professional pianist. He still imagined his wife playing in various world capitals. The ceremony would be immovable. She would appear on the scene with a burst of applauses. The lights of the projectors would dim a little. Facing the public as they held their breath she would take off her blouse and would bow deeply, offering herself to her admirers. Then she would sit down at the piano and the concert would start. Dominique would accompany her on her tours. Each evening the writer would share in one way or another with the spectators, their emotions, maybe their desires. Would he feel jealousy or excitement or both? The ambiguous situation seduced him. He promised himself to ask his wife if she liked the theme of this story. Certainly Laetitia would accept to repeat the experience all the better to inspire him.

12

So the day after, she seemed upset when he spoke to her about their private evening and of that writing project. She avoided the direct questions as well as the allusions, making a face. When he insisted, she redoubled her resistance, frowning ever more fiercely. Disappointed, Dominique could not understand this reaction. Maybe it was part of the play? He had strong doubts about it. He didn't recognize the pianist who bewitched him. Disappointment followed the enchantment. Where was the barbaric, erotic goddess who delighted him making a privileged spectator out of him, a true initiated adept of a cult of womanhood? Vexed, he stopped harassing her and turned his back.

What had happened in Laetitia's mind? Something broke between them, but what? *Had the writer read too much into* a simple incident? Had she regretted the whole episode? Sometimes she was moody, that is true, and unpredictable. Dominique knew this. Was she aware that her husband wasn't insensitive to Nora's charm? The same question came back, nagging him....

He was tired of all these questions. Suddenly

the writer had the urge to go far away, very far off, to a foreign country with a language he didn't speak—maybe Poland? Russia—but he was aware that solitude can offer bad advice. Dominique felt a need to exile himself, even if it would be painful. *Death is coming from the East....* He thought of his mother and of Paul Barbier. His heart sank. Yes, death will always come from the East....There was no escape....

*

Dominique reacted to Laetitia's whim like a spoiled brat who was refused a new toy. Although he was rarely immature regarding her. During their first times together he avoided her on purpose or absented himself without warning, feeling guilty all the same, a rare feeling for him. He wished to make her understand that he also could have changes of heart. His wife wasn't the prudish sort with him generally even if she wouldn't spontaneously accept some of her husband's fantasies, with the pretext that she was "too old now." Who was she anyhow? He hadn't really asked this question before. This time, he wondered. Ten years ago, Laetitia would have had to beg for forgiveness after going AWOL for three days and then launching herself into her little act of *"shedding her leaves"* (he found this term more suggestive and even more sensual than the vulgar English term *striptease*) with Debussy's background music. Or was it perhaps the alcohol's effect? Difficult to say. Laetitia wasn't a woman who would easily lose control of herself, and who, even under the influence of a few glasses of wine, would have let herself go to eccentricities including with him. Dominique would have liked for them to regain a certain complicity that they had once known, trying to preserve it as best as possible

His obsession with Nora returned. He refrained from writing to her. The writer would have loved for the young girl to invite him to Hungary. News from her had been scarce recently. He wrote Jean-Francois Macor to ask him when they would travel to Rome. His secretary answered that the Italian editor was absent for a few weeks. They'd keep him posted; there was no reason to worry.

Apparently nothing had changed for Laetitia. She didn't seem affected by her husband's irritability. She stopped playing the piano after their intimate soiree. Dominique felt some regrets. She had a lot of work to do, but he was persuaded that it wasn't for this reason. The writer forbade himself from interrogating her to avoid bothering her further. He suffered silently finding that her reaction was disproportionate.

*

Finally he received news from Nora who informed him that her Masters was advancing. The student added that she missed him. Dominique was stupidly flattered: she wrote *missed him,* meaning that she excluded Laetitia. In alembicated terms he proposed to come back to Pecs:

I miss you as well.

I'd like to be with you, if that's not too bold....

That was the truth. Nora answered only that the decision belonged to him and that she'd be happy to have him come. Just now she would be busy with exams for some time. After that they would see. She didn't ask about Laetitia. Normally she might have been surprised, even shocked. Yes, he loved Nora, it was certain; how could he doubt it? There was Laetitia, sure, but... Dominique wanted to go join Nora right away, now. Was this reasonable? *Reasonable?* As if this word existed. Was passion reasonable? Questions came one after another, always questions with no answers. What would he say to Nora? That he had fallen in love with her while still in love with Laetitia? That he would leave, abandon everything, including the woman of his life, if she asked him? No, never.

Dominique would never make such a decision.

Laetitia came home. Dominique didn't turn his head in her direction. She didn't say a word either. That was all! It was decided: he'd go to Pecs as soon as possible. The uncertainty maddened him.

*

This little puerile play that empoisoned their relation lasted some weeks and then they ended up by falling into one another's arms. Dominique managed to shoot down his interior demons: the voyage to Hungary would have to be postponed. Nothing was set, however. He didn't know how to obtain forgiveness. Time was too precious to waste like this. Dominique knew that. A little after their marriage he had made a poor attempt at etching the words *Tempus fugit* on an old flat stone half buried in the soil in the garden. With time, the sentence started fading away, while the curse of *Tempus fugit* deepened about them.

Macor asked for two unpublished stories for the *Alla Littera* Press. After being translated by Carlotta, they would appear in an Italian literary magazine. The young woman had asked for the writer's email. She wished to get in touch with Dominique Valarcher to be able to send him her work and eventually inquire about some clarifications on the texts. He could still manage somewhat with Italian from his high school years. Dominique gratefully accepted. He would have liked to go to Rome with Laetitia.... Maybe with Nora?

Nora...his student....

Finally Dominique decided to spend a few days in Pecs. It would be so easy to get around his wife, inventing the excuse of some conference at the University. He didn't hesitate to share his plan with the young Hungarian. Her enthusiastic replies came back momentarily:

That's wonderful!

When?

Sooner, I'm waiting for you!

These appeals dumbfounded him. From the start she didn't say a word about Laetitia. Then he received more lines:

My roommate will be absent for several months.

You could stay at my place if you want.

The writer accepted. He would keep her informed about his arrival. This time his little inner voice kept quiet. Curiously, Dominique deplored this.

*

After some thinking, he went ahead and informed Laetitia as to his travel plans. He told her the truth: next week he'd go for five days to Pecs and would stay with Nora. He didn't regret this disclosure, unable to lie to her. Laetitia didn't reply, nodding only. Paradoxically, Dominique was disappointed by this non-reaction. He presumed that his wife would question him but she was more subtle. He must have doubted it. If Laetitia felt some contradiction she didn't show it. In the family of his wife this was the norm: any emotional manifestation was forbidden, nobody criticized anybody, most of all not a member of the family. More often than not they were in denial. As long as the family was united, at least in appearance, everything was good. It was the reign of the non-said. Laetitia's mother was the tutelary Goddess. She often upheld wrongs without ever turning back to right them. She defended her chicks against the whole world as if they were always ten years of age, all the same criticizing their spouses with pleasure. They all submitted to her rule. The writer was always irritated by this. From the beginning he refused to play the game. He knew all the while it served for nothing *to kick against the pricks*. There must have been the rules like this in many big families. Laetitia had two sisters and a brother. She was the eldest and would never— *never* contest the authority of her mother, even at a grown age. If needed, she would repudiate her husband, and he didn't ignore this fact. The writer remembered one time when Anne-Marie, his mother-in-law, spent a week in Fargette, *at Laetitia's.*

One Sunday morning, a little before eight o'clock, the phone rang waking the couple as they slept leisurely in. It was a far-off uncle of Laetitia's family, passing through Paris. This time, Anne-Marie his mother-in-law just assumed it was okay for her to invite the uncle to their place for lunch, without asking anybody! By what right had his mother-in law, herself an early riser, given their phone number to this unknown man in the first place? Dominique couldn't believe it. His wife didn't make any remark and he kept this to himself. He managed more or less to dissimulate his irritation amid this matriarchal display in all its glory.

Later on, flustered still, Dominique lashed out to Laetitia, "Once—just once in your life you could say 'No' to your mother. It's not too late. It would do you a lot of good, believe me!"

His wife didn't answer. If Dominique was looking for her to blow up, he didn't get it. Laetitia didn't give in to the provocation. At times her silence exasperated him. He would have preferred a clear explanation.

*

Night was falling. Musical notes were coming from the living room. Had Laetitia sat down at the piano? Dominique decided to find out. He slowly opened the door, approaching her with wolf's steps. He made her out in the semi-darkness. She was playing *Gymnopédie n° 1* by Satie, her breasts nude.... Enchanted by the gift, the writer stood still a moment. He would have loved to film this scene. After a few moments of delicious voyeurism, he retreated on tiptoes. She must have noticed that her husband was spying on her, but pretended she didn't. Dominique loved these moments of abandonment. They really weren't so abusive. He would have liked to know the secret thoughts of the *pianist with bare breasts*, as he dubbed her (without letting her in on it). The more curiosity he demonstrated, the more closed toward him was her manner. He couldn't have his way with her.... In that respect they didn't break their implicit rule. Nevertheless Dominique conceded sometimes that it wasn't so disagreeable.

13

Dominique rang the entrance bell at Nora's apartment. She immediately opened the door.

"Hello Dominique. It's so good to see my French author! Come on in. Hurry! I have a gift for you: I translated a poem about Pecs by Weöres Sándor into French, one of the major poets in Hungary. I had it printed on fancy paper."

Nora extended a sheet of paper to him. On it there was a poem of four verses in nice calligraphy followed by the author's name:

Pecs

On top of the town undulated,

The juice of the clocks' sound was dripping

But the moon had eaten everything

The night had fallen.

Weöres Sándor*

Dominique's eyes were full of tears. This time, without hesitating, he squeezed her in his arms. Nora nestled in his arms. He wanted time to stand still, to keep her like that, nestled in like a child in need of affection....

When the writer gave her the *Diorella*, whispering that he wanted to stay "faithful to the tradition," she looked straight into his eyes and lunged for his neck. Dominique was touched: her spontaneity always took him by surprise. He told her so. She blushed.

"The first time I was so afraid that you...that you thought...I don't remember.... We were speaking in friends' terms, I think ?..."

He reassured her with a gesture. Death was no longer boding from the East....

"I almost finished my Master's. I wanted to ask you.... Would you like to reread it, give me your opinion? That would be really helpful!"

"It would be a privilege.... Whatever you want, dear Nora. What do you want?"

"I don't know." She blushed. "Well, maybe...."

The writer looked at her. The student was dressed in a green almond dress. She had attached her hair with ribbons in the same color. Nora looked absolutely stunning. This time he confided in her without hesitation that she resembled Tatiana Samoilova, like two drops of water. She had heard something vaguely about this Soviet actress. Dominique promised to show her photos and bits of her movies on the Internet. With a blush he added that her dress was stunning. He didn't dare say "like yourself." That would be out of place. Moved, Nora gazed in his eyes again. The young girl opened her mouth as she was about to say something and that was all. He noticed that her hands were shaking but abstained from saying anything. She had a silver ring, finely chiseled, on her left ring finger. He complimented it.

"This ring is very old. It belonged to my grandmother," she explained proudly.

"Each time I return to Pecs, the weather is beautiful," he said with a smile. "Thank you so much for the poem. I'll try to learn it by heart, I promise. Thanks also for lodging me, dear Nora. You are truly the fairy of Pecs."

*

The Café Paulus was waiting for them. Some of the students, especially the girls applauded Dominique when he entered. The writer had never felt so serene. He had the impression that he was coming back home. One of the male students kept glancing at Nora, licking his chops at her. Did they know each other? Maybe they were together. Dominique's heart sank. Nevertheless Nora didn't pay any attention to the guy. She was shining.

"I'm really happy," she said again. She maintained the same carefree mood.

Three of Nora's friends approached the table. They wanted a signed book, which the writer gave them with pleasure. In the meantime the student who had been leering at Nora disappeared. Perhaps he was just fascinated by her beauty. Dominique tried to reassure himself. What right did he have to be jealous of Nora's private life? Suddenly he thought of Laetitia. What might she be doing at this particular moment? Did she have tests to correct or was she playing a few piano pieces? He suddenly realized that he didn't know anything about Nora. The student was very discrete about her family, her friends, and her life generally. They looked at each other. Without thinking, he took her hand, wanting to kiss it—then immediately let it go. Dominique apologized. They were in a public place, at elbow room with students, most of whom knew Nora very well. The situation could be embarrassing for her. It seemed to him that a few people around them in particular had raised their voices and made eyes.

Going out of the café he apologized again. Without answering Nora took his hand.

"How about we go for a little walk?"

They walked through the city's streets, hand in hand. At times Nora looked at him and smiled in her usual manner.

It had been a long time, a very long time since Dominique had felt so good. He confessed it to Nora and added, "Yes, you are really the fairy of Pecs."

The world was beautiful and benevolent. It opened its arms for them. Dominique felt he was privileged. In a sense he was.

They came back to the apartment late. Dominique was exhausted from all of the emotions. Dinner had been frugal. He smiled at Nora and without looking at her whispered that she was beautiful and then hurried into his room.

*

That night the writer had a recurrent nightmare, the one that had haunted him some years back: his mother was in a concentration camp. She looked like a mad-woman. She leaned on a man (her first husband?) with a pallid complexion, a worn-out face, who was staggering. One could hear shouts in German, dogs barking, growling.... Soldiers forced people dressed in stripped pyjamas to advance towards the gas chambers hitting them with crosses.

Some were collapsing to the ground.... The beatings doubled in size. His mother was screaming, her eyes out of their sockets: "*Meyn libe! ton nit lozn mir!*" What language was she speaking? It seemed like Yiddish...How could that possible?

He woke up soaked in sweat. Nora sat on the bed, wiping his forehead with a damp towel. The young girl was in her nightgown.

"I was so afraid," she mumbled. "You were groaning in your sleep. I thought I heard you crying and then I let myself into your room... I..."

Dazed, Dominique looked at her; her silhouette was outlined against the moon's light entering through the window. The whiteness of her nightgown hurt his eyes. He could no longer bear to draw the curtains closed due to his night terrors, especially in an unknown room. The young girl was crying silently, and the writer felt ashamed. She bowed and took him in her arms as she would a frightened child. Dominique would have liked to stay a long time like that all cuddled up against Nora. His heart pounded. This time he was sure: he was in love with this young girl, although he knew he'd never give away his secret. Nora and Dominique kept still, huddled to one another. The heart of the world had stopped beating. For Dominique, death would never cease coming from the East. His friend was speaking softly into his ear. She whispered a few words in Hungarian, sang the beginning of a nursery rhyme. He wished to caress her hair but didn't dare; then unable to bear it any longer he fell asleep. The rumors of the past that had almost strangled him had gone silent for now.

"Sleep or the intermittency of nothingness," affirmed Cioran.

14

Nora was just about to have breakfast when Dominique came into the kitchen. The student raised her head and looked at him sadly. She had red eyes, and she looked tired. Dominique felt sheepish like a child caught doing something wrong.

"Please forgive me," he started. "I thought I was finished with all this...."

Nora stopped him with a gesture, making the writer understand that she asked for no justifications on his part. With difficulty she held back a sob [Her voiced quaked difficultly with emotion?]. He would have liked to throw himself at her feet, leaning his head in her lap, becoming again the candid little boy he was before discovering his maternal secret. But what good would this childishness serve for but to trouble her even more? What was he to do? He was at a complete loss.... He simply caressed her face. Nora didn't hold back. She took his hand into hers for a moment.

*

This time Nora didn't accompany the writer to the airport.

"It would have hurt too much," she confided.

He invited her to visit Fargette though without any illusions. Dominique knew that she would never accept for the couple to pay for her voyage. This time again the rain welcomed the writer on his return to France. Laetitia came to pick him up. Maybe it was the rain that blocked their feelings. Each of them avoided the other's eyes. There was a long awkward silence. When his wife asked him how the trip was, he would have liked to answer, "I loved a young girl from a distance but I'll never tell her that."

He didn't open his mouth, pretending he didn't hear the question. He was sure that Laetitia *knew....*

Suddenly in a playful voice, in the voice of a little girl, Laetitia murmured, "Tonight I'll play the piano just for you."

Dominique didn't answer but tried a poor smile. Nora didn't disappear. He would forever at a distance love a young girl to whom he would never confess that love. His obsession with death would never leave him despite the fact that the piano pieces played by the *pianist with bare breasts* could offer him momentary relief. He remembered some verses from a song by Barbara whose title he had forgotten: "Time passes so fast when we love one another. We just saw it passing...." [9]

*

The car finally came to a stop in front of the house. He turned around to face Laetitia. He was under the impression that she was crying, her hands clenched to the wheel. The rain came drumming down. He kissed her hard on the mouth and they both hurried under the downpour into the house.

---

[9] Barbara was a French singer (pseudonym of Monique Serf, 1930-1997)

15

The rain didn't stop for two days. Even Grisette suffered. She was desperately mewing in front of the sliding door of the living room still without deciding to go out.

Dominique got a message from Carlotta. She was asking him for explanations regarding his short stories, notably some specifications on the alternating of verbs in the past simple and the past continuous in a long passage extracted from *Patricia?* The translator took her work seriously, which the writer never doubted. She was giving him the choice between three dates for going to Rome and visiting the offices of *Alla Lettera Press*. Giovanni Mogherini was eager to meet with him: the writer could do a series of conferences, maybe take part in some of the literary TV programs.... Naturally all this would be up to the editor. Yes, of course, he would accept.... The writer thanked the young woman mentioning that he'd be thrilled to see the Italian capital again. He also asked her if she would give his best to Mogherini.

He would have liked to write Nora and give her the news but then thought better. He turned off the computer. He decided not to touch it again today.

Was it an empty promise? Even his little interior voice was silent. For once, Dominique wished that it would bother him again. That was the last straw!

*

Laetitia didn't ask him anything. In any case what could he unveil to her, if not the truth? Once more, even recognizing it wouldn't do them any good to keep bringing up the same old thing, Dominique realized how different their characters were—polarized opposites; he would have liked to know everything, whatever the cost, even if he had to suffer for it. She suffered in silence, at least he supposed so. She had never been too elaborate, he knew this already. So why should he deplore a trait of character that couldn't be changed? At times, truth being told, Laetitia would inquire if he loved her still but that happened less and less. It was he [not she, who needed to be held, to take refuge] who threw himself into her arms, took refuge in her, rarely the opposite. He wondered if his shows of affection sometimes bothered his wife. He mused that if Laetitia had asked him, he wouldn't have gone to Hungary. The coward in him was happy that she hadn't asked him. He was certain that soon he would turn on his computer and check out the messages, searching compulsively for a message from Nora.

When Laetitia was out, he wouldn't even answer the phone. She took to the habit of checking the answering machine when coming back from work. In the evenings in the presence of his wife, he remained silent for long intervals, his eyes vague, lost in some mortifying thought.

16

After turning back home, Dominique feared he would relive the old nightmare. He had wrongly believed he had seen the last of it. It was the same thing: his mother with her eyes out of their sockets, yelling like a madwoman, in the concentration camp where her first husband had disappeared. Dominique thought of consulting a new psychiatrist to help him erase this vision once and for all, or learn how to live with it. To either purpose all of his efforts had been useless. So he gave up on therapy.

Some years back he and Laetitia went to Krakow to meet Agnieszka, a Polish friend who was translating Camus and Ionesco. At the last moment the couple couldn't bring themselves to visit the camp. Was it cowardice? He would have preferred not to ask the question, but afterward he carried a feeling of guilt. He thought of the many buses that unloaded their cargos at Auschwitz, of the high schoolers who were sent there to experience "the duty of memory" (an expression he hated) and see the horror for what it was, so that this sort of tragedy "wouldn't be repeated," as if that were possible. What made these adults believe they were divested with such a mission? What right did they have? What convinced them they were acting for the good of humanity and of these adolescents? In the opinion of Samuel Bronstein, Dominique's former psychiatrist of German origin, who lost part of his family in the deportations, this was a way for the adults to hand their responsibilities over to the younger generation, to throw it in their faces: "Look, younger generation, we show you the genocide of the Jews so that this horror won't be repeated. Now it's your turn. The future belongs to you."

The writer wasn't that far from thinking like Doctor Bronstein. The psychiatrist considered that it would have been better to take these youngsters to Jerusalem, at the Yad Vashem memorial instead of imposing the unspeakable on them.

"I know what you are thinking Mr. Valarcher," he added. "I went myself in pilgrimage to Auschwitz where so many of my family perished. My wife didn't wish to accompany me. I respected her decision, believe me. Do you think I am made of marble in front of all this horror? I am speaking in cognizance of cause, so to speak...."

Dominique was of the opinion that the visit to a concentration camp couldn't be imposed. This choice was a question of individual freedom. Did anyone measure the trauma that could result from this to the adolescents? He spoke about it to a friend who was of a contrary opinion. Melanie was almost mad when the writer asked her if she had ever made this demarche. He just knew she hadn't. It seemed to him that they cheated the high schoolers of their youth by wanting at any cost to impose the inexpressible on them. The young had the right to be carefree even so and the contemporary world wasn't giving them that opportunity at all. Their consciences were being raped.

Dominique wondered what his mother would have thought. He had the intuition that Camille Valarcher hadn't ever visited Auschwitz. She had probably never had the strength. In this respect, also, he was reduced to conjunctures.

Like everybody, on the Internet he had seen those adults who would take pictures obligingly with their mobile phones between the rails leading to death: what indecency! In Prague at the Pinkas synagogue, he would have liked to throw out the tourists dressed in shorts with their colorful caps who stood in line to photograph the lists of the dead Jews being deported.... Once he almost gave a piece of his mind to an

American who noisily called to his girlfriend, "*Hey Babe, come here and look at this!*" [10] so she could see the names written on the walls. While exiting, Dominique's hands were shaking. He was enraged and was talking incoherently. Laetitia wasn't able to calm down this choleric man who was making a fool of himself. When appeased, he wondered if she wasn't ashamed of her husband. At the moment he was about to open his mouth to clarify things, but she whispered looking tenderly at him, "You are the one who is right here." He was grateful. What other woman would have been able to appease him by uttering these simple words of consolation?

---

[10] In English in the original.

17

Dominique couldn't go on like this. He had to find a solution. Laetitia must have been thinking that her husband cheated on her with Nora. Was it so difficult to confess this simple fact to the woman of his life?

"Yes, I'm in love with Nora but we didn't sleep together, I swear to you!"

Maybe the cheating starts at the moment one feels passion for another woman. Dominique would have a hard time reasoning: "All right, she is the age of your daughter!" He didn't ignore the fact that no rational argument could stop his madness.

Finally Nora sent him a message disarming in its sincerity:

Three days have passed since you left, dear Dominique.

Pecs, like my soul, is empty without you.

These simple words troubled him. How should he answer? Something along these lines: "*Forget about me*"? No this was impossible since he could not forget Nora either. He would never accept to answer with such commonplaces: "*The wonderful days spent in your company will remain forever etched in my memory.*" The young girl deserved better than these lyrical take-offs even if this was the truth. Attached to her message, Nora sent him the words of the cradle song she sang for him in French translation; he was touched.

> *Este van már alkonyul,
> Nyuszi füle lekonyul.
> Dorombol a kiscica
> Aludj te is, Dominique!*
>
> *La nuit est déjà tombée,
> Les oreilles du lapin pendent.
> Le chaton ronronne
> Dors, petit Dominique!*
>
> *Night has already fallen
> The rabbit's ears have fallen too*
>
> *The cat is purring quietly
> Sleep, my little Dominique!*

*

Dominique Valarcher was simply surpassed by the last events which had affected—infected maybe his life. He wanted to know what Nora was thinking.

Beyond that touching spontaneity, what were her feelings for him? But really didn't he know them a little? Maybe the student needed a father figure (he would gladly assume this role) or maybe a lover? He was aware that playing the role of a father by procuration could become dangerous. Nora *his* Nora didn't belong to him.

Five years ago the writer undertook a long analysis with Doctor Bronstein that left him with a lot of frustrations but perhaps he had hoped for too much. This time determined to restart it he'd choose a woman therapist: what naivety!

Doctor Bronstein had retired recently but the two of them kept in touch. He knew the writer well and appreciated his books. Maybe he'd accept counselling him. When the phone rang, Dominique hoped that Samuel Bronstein wouldn't answer but he did and recognized his voice: no way to escape. After exchanging some small talk, Dominique bluntly put the question to him and indicated that he would like to see a woman therapist. Doctor Bronstein didn't comment; he gave Dominique the name and the phone number of a certain Marie Dimitrova, who was one of his former students, with a recommendation letter that he'd send to Dominique that day.

"She's Bulgarian by origin," he specified, as if this detail could have some importance. "She's a brilliant woman and a talented visual artist who puts her work on display under a pseudonym. You wouldn't need to know that. Her therapy will suit you perfectly. Tell her that you are contacting her on my recommendation."

He hung up abruptly, leaving the writer disconcerted. He was sure that the old psychiatrist did mention the origins of Marie Dimitrova on purpose. Bronstein knew about the fascination of his patient for Eastern Europe, if from nothing else, just from being a regular reader of his publications.

*

Dominique decided to wait for Laetitia at the University just to surprise her. He saw her from the distance, in front of the amphitheatre, in a grandiose debate with one of her students. The discussion seemed very animated; she was making sweeping gestures, her brow frowning. When she saw her husband she abruptly ended their discussion and rushed towards him. He was surprised. This attitude didn't correspond to the image he had of her. Dominique wondered again if he really knew this woman with whom he had shared his life for so many years. The writer feared that the answer was negative.

Despite his insistence, Laetitia would not allow her husband to take part in one of her courses. What was she afraid of? That he'd discover a very different woman and he'd be disconcerted? That he'd enter her secret garden which she jealously kept to herself? Laetitia took him by the hand. Like Nora, he thought sadly. Dominique abstained from asking her the reason for her irritation with the young man. She wouldn't appreciate his indiscretion. By the way, it doesn't have any importance. Suddenly she turned towards him. "In the opinion of this young imbecile, they should ban Celine[11] from university programs, under the pretext that he was anti-Semitic! What do you think? And to think he was determined to teach French!"

Dominique took his time before answering.

"That student is the one who should be chased away from the University."

Both burst out laughing. Dominique found

----

[11] Pen name of Louis-Ferdinand Destouches, French writer (1894-1961)

her very charming. Laetitia realized his feelings and embraced him passionately, clinging to him. Night was falling. Some stars were shining. Maybe all could begin again between them?

The lovers wandered here and there before going home, browsing the shop windows. In one book-shop window they saw one of his most recent books. Dominique exclaimed, "Here's an author they should ban. He's dangerous for youngsters! Blazes!"

Laetitia and Dominique hurried along down the boulevard, arm in arm, chatting joyously. In the end they dined in a small Greek restaurant *Les Rivages de Chypre* which dated from their student days. It hadn't changed much since then. With the aid of the resinous wine the evening was marked by laughter and endearments. He gazed at her with keen attention. You'd have to be blind not to see her beauty. He whispered that to her. Laetitia answered laughing loudly that she was a married woman, that her husband was very jealous, big and tough! The exact opposite of her actual husband!

Dominique replied, "The hell with him! I love you!"

They both laughed like two children.

*

Laetitia and Dominique had had regained their innocence.

18

The musical voice with Slavic accents of Marie Dimitrova on the telephone disconcerted him. After a few minutes, Dominique hung up without a word. The writer no longer knew if he wanted to start up therapy again or not. Would he ever finish with his phantoms? In Doctor Bronstein's opinion the revelation of his mother's secret was one of the driving forces of his writing. It would be necessary to take some precaution in order to avoid cutting off his inspiration.

"You can't cut off your mother's secret without the risk of destroying yourself, because it is a constituent part of yourself. You need it for writing," affirmed the practitioner. "Remember this aphorism by Nietzsche, *Aus der Kriegsschule des Lebens / Was mich nicht umbringt, macht mich stärker* (From the war's school of life: what doesn't kill me, makes me stronger). Then you have to be worthy of Camille: live following your mother's example. Camille Barbier survived triumphing over death; she showed you the way by loving another man, your father, and giving birth to you! You are the child of Life, Monsieur Valarcher! For God's sake, don't forget this! I am repeating to you, be worthy of Camille!"

One day when the writer blamed himself more than ever, the psychiatrist added, "You reproach yourself for not being able to confide your troubles to your mother. But who knows if Camille wanted this in particular because she never revealed this tragedy to you."

Bronstein interrupted himself a few minutes. Then his face lighted up.

"You know this expression *secret garden?* Well, every garden possesses its own lot of weeds, brambles, nettles, and other bindweeds that the conscientious gardener works and works at to get rid of, only to see them come back up stronger than before.... Candide affirmed that we have to cultivate out garden," Bronstein continued. "There's nothing more true but if one throws away nettles, if I may say, the fanaticism of certain gardeners who are killing that which sometimes we must comprehend.... Be a philosopher-gardener, your equilibrium depends on it.... Voltaire is a good master to think about for a writer, don't you think so?"

*

The lull between Laetitia and Dominique lasted but a short time. A lull is by definition ephemeral. The writer wrote a messy message to Nora where he explained that he was in love with her and wished to disappear from her life in her own interest. Finally he destroyed the note at the last moment just before sending it. One's own to suffer, without making another suffer. For him the alternative came to the same: revealing his passion or dissimulating it meant the same; there wasn't any solution. The writer wondered if he was right to hang up on Marie Dimitrova. He was in dire straits. Two women shared his heart; he could bear the situation no longer. In Pecs Dominique had lived with Nora innocently and euphorically for a few days. His escapade to Hungary was enough to make him happy, to justify his egoism. He deliberately ignored the consequences: the pain that could result for Laetitia and the dissolution of their couple.

Maybe it would be better to think it over a while and get away from Fargette. There was one possibility: Marco Fanfani, an Italian friend, in upper-management in a Franco-Swiss bank had bought a house at Garouze, a medieval village of 300 inhabitants in a remote area of the Nicosia country side. It was a wilderness in the middle of nature, in an enclosed valley. You could only get there on foot. No automobiles were allowed, a locality with a few stores. It was a kind of lost paradise offering itself to the traveler. The inhabitants were vigilant to keep the privileged character of this safe haven.

At the far end of the village, a Franciscan monastery selectively welcomed pilgrims seeking peace and quiet. Dominique could stay there for a while. With his relations, Marco Fanfani could easily obtain a residential permit for the writer. The idea turned round in Dominique's head. It would be good to avoid the summer period prone to an invasion of tourists. He decided to contact Marco without further delay. Let's see...he must have his friend's email in the addresses book if not in the cell phone? Finally, Dominique decided to call him. After some notes from Vivaldi he was invited in English to leave a message, which he did. A few moments later he received a text: *Buongiorno Domenico, everything OK? Extremely busy as usual. Better send me an email.*[12] *Baci.* The writer smiled. His friend liked to juggle languages like French and English, languages that he knew as well as his own. He noted the email of Marco Fanfani

---

[12] In English in the original.

on a piece of paper leaving it on his work table.

Dominique had been acquainted with Marco for a few years. They'd met at an exposition of *17th Century Baroque Europe*. Fanfani acknowledged that he was the patron (mécène) of the event through the intermediary of his foundation

"Mécène I insist," he added. "I'm a banker, a donor and a liberal despot like the Medicis, and definitely not a sponsor, *fa schifo*[*]! This is too vulgar!"

With a sonorous laugh he concluded this declaration of faith, winning Dominique over; the writer baptised him right away Marco *il magnifico*, to the grand satisfaction of the Italian art-lover.

The two men were instant friends. Marco was an intellectual, chiselled and on top of everything Florentine. It sufficed to make *Domenico*, as he was called affectionately by his new friend, fall under the charm of this art-lover whose wife Chiara, loved literature in particular but painted aquarelles as an amateur.

*

Dominique buried his head in his hands. What was he to do? He didn't have a clue, he didn't know anymore...Where was the reality and where the desire? All at once the writer started weeping softly and then more and more loudly. After all he was still a child, who searched for his mother in every woman he loved, and this search would destroy him, this was his intuition. Being in the impossibility to choose between Laetitia and Nora he was making himself unhappy, and was on the verge of making two women unhappy as well.

"You always speak about death in your books," his wife reproached him one day. With a sad smile he answered, "It is because it will have the last word. Remember, Ionesco once wrote: 'Only death will shut me up.'"

Laetitia shrugged her shoulders.

"You're a tragic child. The perfect incarnation of the Russian *nitchev*...like your father. You're always taking refuge in dereliction."

What could be said in response to such a blunt assertion as this one? That genetics explains a lot? Alone, a child could cry while listening to *Sibelius' Concerto for Violin in D minor* interpreted by David Oïstrakh or the sixth movement of *Symphony n°3* by Gustav Mahler conducted by Charles Adler. At that moment all the sadness of the world collapsed on his shoulders leaving him desperate. Dominique would have renounced literature without hesitation to become a composer if only he'd had any talent. At the present time he felt tracked down, vulnerable and abandoned by all. One lone word resumed his thoughts: distress. He would have liked to confide in somebody, in an intimate friend, without ignoring that it was impossible; alone, we are always alone in face of tragedy and adversity.

Suddenly he turned on the computer in a sort of frenzy and sent a message to Marco asking him about Garouze. Without any reason he felt release. This message to his friend was a shout for help, a jump into the unknown. Laetitia...Nora...choosing...the fidelity, the love and a certain security with Laetitia or Nora and a new page to be written.... Did he have any right to take hold in this way of the youth of the Hungarian student, to capture the spontaneity she enveloped him in? Dominique felt old, bitter and tired. He now understood better the pitiful and mocking smiles of the students at Café Paulus. No, decidedly he could not find a solution. He didn't want to be *a tragic child* forever. The writer proved himself to be a coward; it would be his duty to trust this first instinct and write a good-bye letter to Nora explaining to her that he was bogged down in his own contradictions when it came to assuming his responsibilities: *broken identity*.... There was no other way to put it.... He would have to accept the consequences.

*

Marco's answer didn't take long to arrive: his Garouze house would be available for the next four months. Dominique could move in when he wished. It would only suffice to let his "Italian brother" the *magnifico* know in advance. The message was followed by the directions to a neighbor who would give him the keys. How simple things were sometimes, Dominique thought with sadness. The good news should have made him happy or at least appeased him; he had arranged the possibility of a temporary exile for himself, where he could think and maybe write, but once again Laetitia's husband was uncertain.

He put together a few belongings, took a book or two.... What would he say to Laetitia? Whom to ask for advice? Dominique suddenly regretted that he had hung up on that psychiatrist Marie Dimitrova, but maybe it wasn't too late? Nevertheless he was disgusted at the thought of confiding in that stranger, even if she was a therapist. He reproached himself for his pusillanimity. Surely, and the writer knew it, salvation would be found neither in culpability nor in exile.

*

Dominique was losing his certitudes one by one. Never had he fallen so low. At times he estimated that it would have been better to reveal everything to his wife and to Nora. At other times he couldn't see any escape but in flying to Garouze or some other place. What decision could he make? The solution to the problem lay therein, yet somehow not within his reach. The writer acknowledged himself incapable of a decision.

19

When Laetitia returned from the university, she found this simple note on her work-table:

I am leaving. I don't know yet for how long.
I need to think.
Forgive me.
I love you.
Dominique

20

Il rifugio, Chiara and Marco's house was huddled in a vast prairie at the exit from the village. The house was hidden by a hedge of bushy cypresses which kept it away from indiscreet watchers. The place was isolated. The path to it was steep and hard to walk up. One had to climb a small road full of rocks, holes and tall weeds that the couple didn't wish to clean up.

"You have to deserve everything, most of all Paradise," Marco often repeated. The huge garden full of colored flowers and some Mediterranean trees opened towards the valley. His Italian friend had even planted some olive trees brought here from Tuscany. Indeed, it was a paradise.

Some pages of *Noces* by Camus passed through Dominique's mind but he soon chased them from his mind. The beautiful descriptions of that essay weren't of any use to him. He didn't need lyricism right now. What for that *perfumed and acrid sigh of the earth in summer*, celebrated by a book he discovered at 15 years of age in the library of his parents and devoured with great passion? While reading it, Dominique was under the impression that the book was waiting for him, was written especially for him. For the adolescent that he was, Camus had the role of an ideal big brother whom Dominique needed, and would find again and again. Camus took the young reader by the hand in order to guide him towards unknown altitudes.

*

In other circumstances, Dominique would have admired the landscape and especially the monastery whose shape detached itself on the blue sky.

In the cellar of that shepherd's house, there were two refrigerators full of food. He could eat from it liberally. Marco left a few bottles of French and Italian wine for his *dear French brother*. A computer was at the disposition of the guests but Dominique brought his own. The writer didn't have to ask his friend to keep quiet about his stay at Garouze. The Italian esthete was the personification of discretion, and the perfect possible host. Maybe he hadn't even told his wife about this arrangement with Dominique. In any case she would have accepted her husband's reasons.

It was the beginning of June; the air was fresh and clear. Dominique flung himself onto a sofa. A few years back Chiara and Marco bought this old stone abandoned house for almost nothing. They fixed it up, making it almost comfortable. The Italian couple visited this haven of peace regularly, their refuge, to forget for the moment the worries of their hectic life. Chiara loved to paint the surrounding landscapes and then offered reproductions to their friends. She had the habit of annotating the books she brought to the Refugio. Their guests were allowed to borrow the books as they pleased, which they liberally did. Dominique could count on the devotion of the couple, always ready to satisfy the needs of their friends.

*

The writer thought of Laetitia. His wife had surely discovered his note by now. The reasons for his "eloping" may seem strange to her, at least partially. Did she think her husband had left her for Nora? The writer was obsessed by this question. He didn't want to make her suffer. Maybe she suspected his successive torments? Dominique blamed himself for his weakness but now it was too late; he didn't have the force to retrace his steps and take his wife into his arms asking for forgiveness. He loved her as always, he was certain, but there was Nora. Nora, whose sentiments towards him the writer ignored even now.

He discovered how cowardly he was; where would he end up, running away like that? In this particular moment Dominique would have loved to share this refuge at the world's end with the student, though this would have made him feel like a child with his hand in the cookie jar. They could have worked in peace on that project of interviews.... But who could say how far this intimacy would take them? He didn't dare consider it.

Who wrote that implacable aphorism "To love is to suffer and to make someone else suffer?" This assertion could have been pronounced by one of his characters. Perhaps this was the case. Dominique should have given some news to Jean-Francois Macor and to that Italian translator and to many others...but he didn't have the strength to do so. One was always alone, his back against a wall, incapable of making a decision when circumstances demanded it.

*

Nothing will ever be as before, Dominique felt. But nevertheless, the weather was so good...*The tragic child* went out into the garden. The silence barely perturbed by a bird's trill, and the obstinate buzzing of the insects, oppressed him. Perhaps the writer could still go back summoning the two women of his life here, at this house in Garouze, explaining himself, trying finally to justify himself, facing them; maybe together they would be able to find a solution, but Dominique knew already that he was incapable. Paradise didn't exist.

So was this at last the meaning of cowardice? Were his books' heroes this similar to himself? Dominique raised his eyes towards the sky before closing them for a long time; why was it that it was always too late? He felt assaulted by contradictory thoughts. The writer had a feeling that the situation couldn't be solved. Yes, paradise didn't exist.

Suddenly he rushed back into the interior of the house and slammed the windows' wood shutters closed.

Once in the shade, Dominique oriented himself by groping before falling heavily on the sofa which made a moaning sound. Dominique didn't move. He would stay still like this without doing anything. He would have liked to die then and there.

*

All at once he had the sensation that night was falling. Dominique closed his eyes once more, and wished that his heart would finally stop beating.

NOTES

Introduction

   * Nitchevo: nothing. Fatalist and resigned attitude characteristic to a Russian soul.

Chapter 3

   * Pörkölt: ragout meat with paprika accompanied by pasta or mashed potatoes.

   † Halászlé: fish soup made of various fishes mostly carp, and seasoned with paprika—a Southern Hungarian speciality notably from Pecs and Szeged.

   ‡ Blöff Bisztro: Pecs restaurant specialised in Mediterranean cooking, such as fish and shell fish.

Chapter 7

   * Bikavér: red wine known by the name "bull's blood" celebrated Hungarian wine great with meaty dishes.

   † Lecsó: Dish cooked with onions, tomatoes, peppers and bacon sometime accompanied by rice.

   ‡ *Köszönöm, barátaim. Mindig szívemben éltek majd.*: Thank you my friends. You will always stay in my heart.

Denis Emorine

Chapter 10

    * Ты наш: you are one of us.

Chapter 13

    * Original version of the poem by

        Weöres Sándor:

        Pécs

        A hullámos város felett

        harangok hang-leve folyt.

        De mind fölitta a Hold,

        hogy éjszaka lett.

Chapter 17

    * French translation of the Hungarian cradle

        song: Monique Palomares.

        www.mamalisa.com/?t=fs&p=3296

Chapter 18

    * *Fa schifo*: it's rotten

My gratitude goes to my friend, the poet and translator Károly Sándor Pallai who kindly answered my questions about Hungary.

Equally, I am grateful to the Soviet actress Tatiana Samoïlova (1934-2014) whom I did know very well, without meting her in person ever.

ABOUT THE AUTHOR

Denis Emorine is the author of short stories, essays, poetry, and plays. He was born in 1956 in Paris and studied literature at the Sorbonne (University of Paris). He has an affective relationship to English because his mother was an English teacher. His father was of Russian ancestry.

His works are translated into several languages. His theatrical output has been staged in France, Canada (Quebec) and Russia. Many of his books (stories, drama, poetry) have been published in Greece, Hungary, Romania, India, Japan, South Africa and the USA.

Writing, for Emorine, is a way of harnessing time in its incessant flight. Themes that re-occur throughout his writing include the Doppelgänger, lost or shattered identity, and mythical Venice (a place that truly fascinates him). He also has a great interest in Eastern Europe.

A checklist of JEF titles